STEPSISTER
from the
PLANET WEIRD

by Francess Lantz

Random House 🏠 **New York**

For Renee Cho—
Thanks for your help navigating the Planet Weird

http://www.randomhouse.com/

RL: 5.2

Library of Congress Cataloging-in-Publication Data
Lantz, Francess Lin, 1952–
Stepsister from the Planet Weird / by Francess Lantz.
p. cm.
Summary: Although twelve-year-old Megan usually discounts
her younger brother's outer space fantasies, she is not so certain
that he is wrong when he suggests that the unusual man with
whom their surfer mother has fallen in love and his seemingly
perfect daughter are aliens.
ISBN 0-679-87330-9 (pbk.) – ISBN 0-679-97330-3 (lib. bdg.)
[1. Extraterrestrial beings–Fiction. 2. Stepfamilies–Fiction.
3. Remarriage–Fiction. 4. Parent and child–Fiction.]
PZ7.L2947St 1997
[Fic]–dc20 96-43938

Reprinted by arrangement with Random House, Inc.
Printed in Canada.
10 9 8 7 6 5 4 3 2

ONE

Ariel's Diary

Writing.

What an odd and distasteful concept. It's so flat, so linear, so...solid.

My father—Daddy, as he wants me to call him—insists that I write in this journal in order to practice thinking and writing in the language known as English. The point, he says, is to help me fit in here on Earth. But why? I don't want to fit in, and I don't understand why I should try. After all, I'm not an Earthling and I never shall be. I'm a Zircalonian and proud of it.

Oh, how I miss Zircalon-6. The vast plains of purple grasses, the yellow sky, the hot, dry air. And the people. Of course, they aren't people exactly—not human beings, anyway—but there is no other word I can find in English to describe them. "Creatures" sounds so crude, and "aliens"...well, they're not alien to me. The Zircalonians are my tribe, my species (I'm finding these words in a book my father gave me called a thesaurus), my soulmates.

At night I dream I'm on Z-6 again. My body is no longer flesh and bone, no longer solid and unchangeable. Instead I am once again a ball of beautiful pink gas laced with nerve sensors, floating gently beside my friends, telepathically perceiving their thoughts, feeling them perceive mine.

And then I dream I'm transforming myself into a liquid state. Ah, what joy! Zircalonian adults—those who are over two hundred Earth years old—consider it immature to spend so much wet time, but what do they know? I may be only a youth of ninety-nine years, but I can't imagine anything more thrilling than joining my friends, all of us in a liquid state, as we rush through the maze of tubes at TubeWorld.

My father—sorry, <u>Daddy</u>—says there's an Earth equivalent of tube riding. It's called surfing. But how much fun can it be if you have to remain in a solid state? To slide through the water is one thing. To actually <u>be</u> moving water…that is quite another.

I had to stop a moment to clean my eyes. An odd thing happens here on Earth when I feel sad. Salty drops of water, called tears, issue forth from my eyeballs and drip down my face. How can it be that the act of creating water—an expression of gaiety and joyous abandon on Z-6—is a sign of sorrow here? It is so peculiar, but then everything about my body is peculiar now.

I stare in the mirror at my smooth pinkish-beige

flesh, my flat face, the horrible yellow hair that grows from my scalp. I am grotesque, and my father is just as ugly. And yet he seems to accept the way we look, even to like it. Who can understand such a thing?

But then Daddy (see? I'm learning) always was different. Even when I was a small child, I knew there was something wrong with him. Rather than remaining in a gaseous state—or even the liquid state so beloved of youth—my father always preferred to be solid. How well I remember my mother criticizing him. "What is wrong with you, Fffleeboxx?" she would think angrily (no need for the slow, cumbersome speech that Earthlings use; Zircalonians need only think their mind to be perceived). "No one chooses to be solid!"

Of course, even on Z-6, we are sometimes called on to assume a solid state. Since nothing exists on the planet except sand, purple grass, and floating gases, we must do our part to transform ourselves into the solid objects we need—the tubes at TubeWorld, the balloon-like pods that protect us from the seasonal wind-storms, the spaceships that take us across the universe in search of life-sustaining helium. To temporarily transform ourselves into useful objects is our duty. But no one finds pleasure in solidity—no one, that is, except my father.

That is why my parents eventually ended their commitment to each other. And why Daddy took a position with the Helium Exploration Corps, transporting helium from other parts of the universe back to our home planet. For two years, he traveled the galaxy with the

HEC, returning home only sporadically. And then...

Once again my eyes produce salt water as I remember the dreadful day my mother was caught in an unexpected windstorm and her molecules were fatally separated. My father returned home to fetch me, and I was forced to join him on his travels. How displaced I felt. How lost. Most of Daddy's assignments were on barren, uninhabited planets in the far reaches of the galaxy. I was often alone, and always lonely.

But then, on that first glorious visit back to Z-6, I met and fell in love with...how can I translate his name into English? Ffffoopp (that's the closest I can come). Oh, the hours we spent probing each other's thoughts, floating over the purple grasses, tumbling through the tubes at TubeWorld, playing ever-more-intimate mind games!

We had a mere twelve moons together before Daddy was sent to the Z-6 settlement on GrRp. Oh, horrid GrRp. Hated GrRp. It is because of the GrRpians—and the dreadful receiving machines they built to pick up television transmissions from Earth—that we are here today.

I shudder when I recall the first time my father viewed Earth TV. His gaseous form became instantly wet with excitement.

"Look!" he thought to me. "See the Earth creatures with their solid forms and bright colors! Are they not fabulous?"

I watched the screen. I saw Earthlings sitting in boxes cluttered with solid objects. They wore fabric draped over their skin. Noises were coming out of the holes in their faces. With awkward, jerky motions they lifted red cans and poured fizzy brown liquid into their face holes.

"This world is too heavy, too full of things, too loud," I thought. "The creatures are distinct, solid, and separate. I am unmoved."

But my father was transfixed. Day in and day out, he stared at the receiving screen. He forgot all about the helium he had come to GrRp to collect. Finally, the HEC reprimanded him and ordered us to return home. It was then that Daddy allowed me to perceive the plan he had been forming in his mind. We were never returning to Zircalon-6. Instead, we were to assume the shape of human beings and settle on planet Earth, in the geographic region known as Southern California.

I was appalled. I was distraught. I was flummoxed. But what could I do? I tried to convince my father that he was making a massive error, that Earth was a crude and primitive place lacking the unity, the serenity, the gaseous tranquillity of Z-6. But it was no use. Clearly, his already unstable mental state had been completely unbalanced by his continuous exposure to the horrific hubbub of Earth TV. Indeed, he seemed to be convinced that life on Earth would be exciting, stimulating. Fun, even.

And so here we are. Everything has happened so fast, I can barely assimilate it. After watching a few hours of medical shows on the receiving screen to learn about the inner workings of the human body, my father transformed himself into what he considered to be a healthy, attractive human being.

Since I have no interest in Earthly bodies, my father dreamed up the details of my human form and I reluctantly transformed myself to his specifications. He thought up our names, too: Cosmo for him, Ariel for me, and Cola for our second names (after that vile brown liquid in the red cans).

Now we too live in a box (called an apartment), drape outlandish fabrics (known as clothes) over our solid bodies, and insert food substances into the holes in our faces (that is, we eat meals with our mouths). But our real food is helium, of course, which we purchase by the tank and breathe into our lungs. It has become my only joy, since all other pleasure is denied me.

My hand trembles as I write; my eyes make salt water and my nose leaks. I try to transform myself into a gaseous state, but I cannot. Since arriving on Earth, I have been trapped in this solid, heavy body, able to change my shape only slightly with the greatest physical and mental effort (and only after ingesting a large amount of helium). To cheer me up, Daddy reminds me that human bodies are ninety-eight percent water. But what good does it do me when the liquid is held prisoner inside a disgusting bag of skin?

Even worse, I can no longer perceive my father's thoughts, and he cannot perceive mine. In fact, I can't even see into the minds of other humans, simple though their thought processes may be. Why? I do not know, nor does my father. All I do know is that I am alone, thinking my own miserable thoughts, unable to communicate except by expelling air through my moving mouth. Or even worse, by scratching the point of a pen across paper, as I'm doing now.

But the worst thing of all (can there be more?) is that my father doesn't seem to mind. In fact, he is positively delirious with happiness. He spends his days exploring the city, returning home each evening with his arms full of absurd objects that he has discovered and purchased—cotton balls; potted plants; cassette tapes, which transmit a variety of chaotic sound waves; a pair of plastic, chattering teeth. Then he spends the evening watching TV, playing with his new possessions, and inserting food into his face hole.

My only hope—the one thing that sustains me—is that my father will eventually tire of this frenetic, foolish planet and return to Zircalon-6. I try to be an example to him, to remind him of everything soft and serene and beautiful he has left behind. But it is so difficult to be soft and serene inside this lump of flesh that is—

I must stop writing. Daddy has returned home and is calling for me. He sounds positively atwitter. I cringe to think what outlandish consumer goods he has purchased today.

Oh, dreariness and dread! Oh, muddle and misery! I was certain life could not get any worse, but I was wrong.

Because we arrived on Earth with only a small amount of local currency (procured on the intergalactic black market), my father went into the world today determined to find some form of human work. Instead, he has returned home with the announcement that he has met the most lovely, the most intelligent, the most charming female human being on the planet. We leave tomorrow to visit her at her dwelling, in a geographic location known as Playa Vista, approximately three hours north of here.

Oh, purple plains of Zircalon-6! Oh, my beloved Ffffoopp! Will I ever see you again?

TWO

"Hey, Mom, what's for dinner?"

My mother glanced up from the kitchen counter as I walked in the front door and wiped my wet, sandy feet on the rug. Unlike most mothers, sandy feet and dripping bathing suits have never bothered her. Neither has dust, clutter, or much of anything else.

"Peanut butter and jellybean tacos," she replied, then smiled. "How was the beach, Megan?"

"Awesome!" I tossed my towel in the general direction of the laundry room. "I met the boy of my dreams."

My little brother, Mickey, skipped through the door after me and began bouncing on the living room sofa. "You mean that surfer dude in the black and purple wetsuit? The one you were talking to after you rescued me?"

"Rescued you?" Mom exclaimed. "What happened?"

"No big deal," I said quickly. "Mickey went out at

Pelican Point on his crocodile raft and drifted into the surf. I paddled out on my surfboard and towed him in before he got pounded. And then Cutter Colburne walked up and said what I'd done was impressive. That was his exact word—impressive. He said—"

"Mickey, what on earth were you thinking?" Mom demanded, turning toward my little brother.

"I wasn't on Earth," he replied. "I was pretending I'd just made an emergency landing on Venus in my space capsule."

"Give it a rest," I told him. "Can't you at least *try* to talk like a normal six-year-old?"

But I knew it was hopeless. Mickey is not normal. I mean, the kid is absolutely obsessed with outer space. He reads about it, watches videos about it, and even talks in his sleep about it. In fact, his one and only desire in life is to become an astronaut so he can travel to other planets and meet alien beings.

Mom shook her head and sighed. "You have to be more careful, Mickey. And Megan, you need to keep a closer eye on your brother."

"Aw, Mom, it was bad enough I had to take him with me in the first place. Besides—"

Mom cut me off with a wave of her hand. "Let's not argue. The tacos are ready and I'm famished." She walked into the living room and pushed aside a jumble of junk mail and old newspapers to set the plates down on the coffee table. Gnarly, our big sandy-colored mutt, trotted over, ready to lick up any morsels of food that might fall his way.

I joined Mom and Mickey on the sofa and took a bite of my taco. I was still sailing high from my close encounter with Cutter. He had talked to me. He had smiled at me. Could true love be far behind?

Okay, maybe not. After all, he was an eighth grader and a total hunk, not to mention the unofficial leader of the school's surf club, the Stingrays. I, on the other hand, was a lowly sixth grader. Still, I could dream, couldn't I?

"What a day!" Mom exclaimed, throwing her arm over the back of the sofa. "A spectacular day, in fact."

My mother is a former professional surfer who runs a beach shop called High Tide Ocean Sports. Every spring and fall she goes down to a big surf-wear show in San Diego to buy merchandise for the store—everything from bathing suits to boogie boards. Today she had driven down for the fall show.

"But I thought you hated surfwear shows," I said. "You always complain about the crowds and the noise and the—"

"This one was different," she insisted. "Megan, you know how you met the boy of your dreams today?" She smiled. "Well, so did I."

I stared at her. Mom is not exactly the romantic type. I mean, since she and my dad got divorced three years ago she's dated four, maybe five, guys, none of them for more than a month.

"What are you talking about, Mom?" I figured she was joking, so I waited for the punch line.

My mother stared off into space and let out a dreamy sigh. "Kids," she announced, "I'm in love. His name is Cosmo Cola."

"Cosmo *what?*" Mickey asked with a giggle.

"Cosmo Cola," Mom replied. "Cos for short. I know it's an unusual name, but then he's an unusual man." She turned to me. "Do you know what he was doing when we met?"

I didn't answer. I was still reeling from Mom's announcement that she was in love.

"He was sniffing a wetsuit," Mom said, not waiting for my reply. "I asked him what was up. I thought maybe he was a buyer and he'd found some trick for testing the durability of neoprene. But he said he'd never smelled anything like it before."

"What? Neoprene is just rubber," I said. "Who's never smelled rubber?"

"Who'd want to?" Mickey pointed out.

Mom smiled. "Cos has a childlike curiosity about things that I find really refreshing. Unlike most men, he isn't the least bit jaded."

"What does he do for a living?" I asked suspiciously. Based on what I'd heard about this Cosmo dude so far, I figured he was probably an escapee from a mental hospital.

Mom hesitated. "Well...nothing right now. He just moved to San Diego from a little town in northern Canada. Apparently, it's so small it isn't even on the map. He spent his entire life there until recently, so it's no wonder he finds California fascinating."

"Maybe he's an alien, sent here to study Earthlings and their ways." Mickey's eyes brightened at the idea. "Is there anything weird about the way he looks—green skin, antennas, stuff like that?"

"Right, Mick," I said, rolling my eyes. I turned to Mom. "What was this Cos guy doing at a surfwear show anyway? Aren't they only open to buyers from surf shops and department stores?"

"He was just walking by. He said he caught a glimpse of all the wild multicolored clothing and he was mesmerized." She started laughing. "We went out to lunch, and you should have seen him. It was almost as if he'd never tasted food before. I mean, he ate with such gusto."

She sat back on the sofa and sighed. "Kids, I think you're really going to like him."

"We're going to meet him?" Mickey asked.

Mom nodded. "He's driving up tomorrow. I'm going to help him look for a job. Then he's coming over for dinner."

"A job?" I repeated. "But I thought you said he lived in San Diego."

"He does, but he's thinking of moving to Playa Vista." She grinned. "Wouldn't that be wonderful?"

I stared at Mom. I'd never seen her like this. Her eyes were sparkling, her cheeks were flushed, and her voice was practically squeaking with excitement. I frowned. What if she really was in love with this

Cosmo dude? And what if he moved to town and started hanging out at our house all the time? Or even—heaven forbid—moved in?

The thought hit me like a wipeout on a ten-foot wave. I didn't want my life to change. I liked living with Mom and Mickey, eating peanut butter and jellybean tacos, staying up past my bedtime to watch late movies, ditching school when Mom got the notion to go on a surfing safari up the coast.

Okay, so maybe we didn't have much money, our roof leaked in twelve different places when it rained, and I hadn't been able to find two matching socks in years. Who cared? I was happy, and I didn't want some whacked-out lumberjack from the frozen North turning my life upside down.

I got up and walked to the window. The sun was beginning to set over the ocean, turning the sky a gorgeous swirl of red and purple. Gazing at it, I felt the bad thoughts slipping away. *Get a grip, Megan,* I told myself. *Mom is going to* date *this guy, not* marry *him. In a couple of weeks she'll realize he's a flake, and that will be that.*

I went back to the sofa and finished my taco, confident that everything was going to be fine. Little did I know how wrong I'd turn out to be.

When school ended the next day, I was walking on air. That was because Cutter Colburne and I had passed each other in the hallway between fifth and sixth periods, and he had actually talked to me. "Hey," he'd said, throwing me a casual wave, "it's you. The surfing lifeguard."

I glanced at my two best friends, Robin and Tara, who were walking beside me. Was I hallucinating? When I saw them giggle, I knew that I wasn't. Cutter Colburne, surf god of Playa Vista Middle School, was acknowledging my existence. In public.

"Hi," I gulped. I seemed to have forgotten how to breathe.

"You surf Pelican Point a lot?" he asked.

"All the time."

"Me too. According to the surf report on KJJE, there's a storm moving up the coast. We should see a big swell coming through this weekend."

I shook my head. "The storm got stalled down in Baja. At least that's what they're saying on SurfLine."

"SurfLine," he said. "What's that?"

"A new 1-900 number I read about in *Surf Scene*. They update their surf report every two hours."

"Outstanding. What's the number?" I told him, and he jotted it down on the front of his notebook. Then he smiled at me. "What's your name?"

"Megan. Megan Larsen."

"I'm Cutter. See ya in the surf." Then he walked away, leaving me weak in the knees and grinning from ear to ear.

I was still grinning when I picked up Mickey at his elementary school and drove him home on the back of my bike. As I pedaled, I fantasized about Cutter. Our conversation would lead to longer conversations. Soon we'd go surfing together. Then one day he'd tell me he loved me and ask me to join the Stingrays.

Whoa, girl, I warned myself. *Slow down.* The Stingrays had never admitted a female to their ranks, let alone a sixth grader. Still, it was a terrific fantasy, and as I turned my bike into our driveway, I could almost believe it might come true.

A deep, booming voice brought me back to reality. "You must be Megan and Mickey!"

I looked up to see a tall, round, bearlike man standing in the doorway of our house, grinning. He had curly brown hair, a thick beard, and twinkling green eyes. He was wearing baggy, multicolored pants, a flaming pink Bugs Bunny sweatshirt, and heavy fur-lined boots that looked way too warm for the seventy-degree weather.

"And you must be Cos," I said, desperately hoping I was wrong.

"Right on the first try," he boomed happily. "You'd make a good game show contestant. Do you like game shows? *Wheel of Fortune* is my favorite."

"Oh," I said, climbing off my bike.

"Where's Mom?" Mickey asked. "What's for dinner?"

"Your charming mother is in the bathroom with my daughter," Cos replied. "She—"

"Daughter?" I gasped. "Mom never said you had a kid." My mother had never dated a man with children before—at least not that I knew of. In any case, we'd never been forced to meet them.

"That's because she didn't know," Cos said merrily. "But I think they're hitting it off nicely. Come on in and meet her."

Swell, I thought, trudging into the house. As if things weren't bad enough, *now* I was going to be forced to make conversation with some nerdy backwoods girl from Beaver Brains, Canada. I turned to Mickey and whispered, "She's probably a bookworm with body odor and no social skills."

Mickey giggled, but Cos went on talking, completely oblivious. "We were cleaning off the barbecue grill—we're having hamburgers, Mickey—and your dog jumped up and knocked the hose out of my hand. Ariel got sprayed right in the face." He laughed loudly, an explosive *Har, har, har* that made me cringe. "She's in the bathroom drying off."

Out of the corner of my eye, I noticed something moving near the ceiling. I looked up to see a dozen red and blue balloons bouncing gently against the light fixture. Cos followed my gaze and smiled.

"I brought balloons," he said cheerfully. "And diet cola. Do you like balloons? I do." He picked up a can of soda from the cluttered coffee table and took a big gulp. "Mmm-mmm, good!" he exclaimed, then let out a loud, satisfied burp.

I stared at Cos. Was this guy for real? Mickey was staring at him, too. "Are you from outer space?" he asked suddenly.

Cos gasped and took a step backward. His mouth fell open and the can of cola dropped from his hand. It hit the coffee table and splattered in all directions.

At the same moment, a high-pitched shriek rocked the house. I spun around just in time to see a girl about my age come running into the living room. Her eyes were wide and her hair was flying behind her.

"Wind! Wind!" she screamed, throwing herself under the coffee table and covering her head with her arms. "We're all going to die!"

THREE

My mother appeared a moment later, holding a hair dryer in her hand. She looked stunned. "Where's Ariel? I offered to dry her hair and she ran out of the room."

"Oh, gosh, I, uh—" Cos laughed in embarrassment. "I should have told you. When Ariel was just a child, a...uh...hurricane hit our little Canadian town. Ariel was playing outside and she was blown clear across a field. It was very traumatic for her. Ever since that day, whenever she's near strong winds...well, you see what happens."

I looked at Ariel, cowering under the coffee table. "I thought hurricanes only happened in the tropics."

Cos slapped his forehead with the heel of his hand. "Did I say hurricane? I meant tornado." He crouched down beside the coffee table. "Come out, Ariel, darling. Everything's going to be all right."

Slowly, Ariel crawled out and stood up. Now I was able to get a good look at her. What a shock! I had been picturing a miniature version of Cos, but this girl had flawless white skin, shiny blond hair that fell almost to her waist, big violet-blue eyes, and a body that was straight out of a fashion magazine. In a word, she was a knockout.

"You poor dear!" my mother exclaimed. "I'm so sorry I frightened you." Mom reached out to touch Ariel, but she pulled away and walked out of the room.

Cos laughed nervously. "She's still upset. I'll go talk to her."

Suddenly I noticed the puddle on the coffee table. It was from Cos's can of cola, the one he'd dropped before Ariel ran into the room. The brown liquid was seeping into the sheets of paper nearby.

"My social studies report!" I cried, grabbing the papers and shaking them wildly. "It's ruined!" I ran into the kitchen, ripped off a paper towel, and began blotting the papers. Cos followed after me.

"This report is due tomorrow," I cried. "Now I have to copy the entire thing over!"

"I'm sure it was an accident, Megan," Mom said, joining me in the kitchen. She took the report out of my hand and held it up to the light. "It doesn't look that bad. I'll write a note to your teacher, okay?"

I rolled my eyes. "Oh, all right." But I wasn't about to forgive Cos. So far, he and his loony daughter had caused nothing but trouble. *Why don't they go back to where they came from?* I thought irritably.

If Cos knew how I felt about him, he didn't show it. He turned to Mickey, who had joined us all in the kitchen. "Mickey," he asked hesitantly, "what...I mean, why did you ask if I was from outer space?"

"Oh, Mickey, you didn't!" Mom exclaimed with a laugh. She turned to Cos. "Don't mind my silly son," she said. "He's watched *E.T.* and *Star Wars* so many times, he's convinced that every light in the sky is a UFO and every person he meets is a space alien."

"Well, *are* you?" Mickey demanded.

Cos laughed heartily. "Of course not. I'm a human being, just like all of you."

Well, not exactly like us, I thought, *because we're normal.* But I didn't say it.

We heard a sound from the living room. "It's Ariel," Mom whispered to me. "Go talk to her, Megan. Be nice." I started to protest, but Mom shot me a look that said, *Go!*

With a sigh, I turned and walked into the living room. What I saw made me stop dead in my tracks. Ariel was holding a red balloon. She'd put the open end in her mouth and was sucking up the helium.

I stepped back and Ariel saw me. Her eyes grew wide. "Megan," she squeaked in a high-pitched cartoon voice. "I...er...I did not perceive you there."

She sounded so silly I burst out laughing. "I saw someone suck helium in a movie once and his voice got all high and goofy, but I never knew if it was for real or just a special effect." I walked over to her. "I guess it's for real."

Ariel looked surprised. "There are others who inhale helium?" she squeaked.

"That's a weird question." I stared at her. "It can't be good for you. Why are you doing it?"

Ariel gazed at a spot just above my head. She seemed incapable of looking me in the eye. "Errr..."

What the heck was the matter with this girl? I wondered. Maybe along with being caught in a tornado, she'd also been hit by lightning.

"Well?" I prompted. "Why are you doing it? A science report for school or something?"

"Yes, that is the reason," she said in a voice that was now normal. Actually, it wasn't exactly normal. It was soft and breathy and sweet. Almost musical.

I suddenly preferred the cartoon helium voice.

"Come and get it," my mother called from the back door. "We're eating outside at the picnic table."

Gratefully, I hurried through the kitchen and out to the backyard. Mom was standing at the barbecue, flipping the burgers. Gnarly was at her feet, drooling. Mickey was sitting on his knees at the picnic table, holding his fork in one fist and his knife in the other. Cos was beside him in exactly the same position, looking like an overgrown six-year-old.

A moment later, Ariel wafted through the back door. That's the only way I can describe it. Her movements were slow, fluid, graceful. And so light. I mean, you could barely notice her feet touching the ground. It was almost as if she were floating.

"I hope you're hungry," Mom said, reaching for the spatula and sliding it under a sizzling hamburger.

Ariel looked at the burger and wrinkled her perfect little nose. I felt a surge of anger. Granted, Mom's cooking wasn't gourmet. But what was Ariel used to—five-star French restaurants?

"Attention," Ariel said. "That animal is about to jump up and procure your food substance—"

Gnarly leaped up and snatched the hamburger right off the spatula. "Bad dog!" Mom scolded as he disappeared around the corner of the house.

Cos looked positively delighted. "I like dogs!" he exclaimed. "Such infantile minds inside such powerful bodies. It's fascinating!"

Mom laughed and went back to serving the burgers, but I wasn't laughing. Ariel had warned us about Gnarly *before* he even jumped.

"Ariel, how did you know Gnarly was about to grab that burger?" I asked her.

She gazed at a spot over my head again. "I...er..."

"Just a good guess," Cos said with a smile.

"An amazing guess, I'd say. Are you really into dogs or something?" I asked her.

Ariel frowned. "My form is much larger than that of your dog. I do not think I could fit *into* him."

Was she teasing me? "What I meant was—"

"Here we go," Mom said, setting a plate of hamburgers on the table. "Help yourselves."

Cos eagerly reached out and took two. He stacked both burgers on his bun.

Mom laughed. "I like a man who enjoys his

food." She handed him a platter piled with tomatoes, lettuce, and pickles.

Cos piled some of each on his burger. Then he added baked beans, potato salad, tortilla chips, ketchup, mustard, mayonnaise, salt, and pepper. When he was finished, he could barely fit it into his mouth. Ignoring the ketchup oozing out the sides, he took a huge bite. Grease dribbled down his chin. "I like eating!" he exclaimed as he chewed.

Mickey giggled and began to make his own smaller version of the Cosburger. I looked over at Ariel's plate. It held nothing but a slice of tomato, a scrap of lettuce, and small dabs of ketchup, mustard, and mayo. She picked up her fork and began to daintily eat the mayonnaise.

"Don't you want a hamburger, Ariel?" Mom asked.

"I don't like hamburgers," she said.

"Oh, dear. Can I get you something else? A tuna sandwich maybe? Or grilled cheese?"

"I don't like tuna sandwiches or grilled cheese."

"Ariel's not a big eater," Cos said between mouthfuls.

"Food is messy," she explained. "And it tastes odd."

"What is this yummy green thing?" Cos asked, completely unconcerned about his rude daughter. He reached under the bun and pulled out a pickle.

"You never had a pickle?" Mickey asked.

"Uh...they don't have pickles in northern

Canada," Cos said. Just then, Gnarly sauntered around the corner of the house.

"Look who's back," Mickey announced, pointing. As he did, his elbow knocked against his glass of grape juice, sending it splattering across the table and onto Ariel's blouse.

She let out a shriek and jumped to her feet in horror. Mom let out an exasperated sigh. "Megan, take Ariel inside and lend her one of your blouses, will you?"

Oh, joy. "Come on," I said, heading into the house. Ariel floated after me. It was like being followed by a cloud.

I walked into my room and opened my closet. "Here," I said. "Pick anything you want. Except my Pipeline T-shirt. That's special."

"Why?" she asked, unbuttoning her blue blouse. She was actually wearing a wool sweater underneath. Just looking at her made me sweat.

"Because I bought it in Hawaii. We went there on vacation last year. Check it out." I pointed to a series of snapshots I had taped up on the wall. There was one of Mom surfing Pipeline, another of me surfing the inside reef at Sunset Beach, and one of Mickey building a sand space module.

Ariel stared at the photos, mesmerized. "What is she doing?" She pointed to the photo of Mom.

"Surfing," I said. "I guess they don't do that in northern Canada, huh?"

"At home I did not need a board," she said, gazing dreamily. "At home I was one with the water."

"What do you mean? You swim? Bodysurf?"

"Something like that," she said. "Back home things are different. Back home, it is beautiful."

Well, excuse me, I felt like saying. *I'm sorry our crummy little country doesn't please your royal highness.* Instead, I just grunted, picked up her stained blouse, and marched into the bathroom. I tossed it into the sink and turned on the water.

Ariel followed. She stared at the running water a moment with a zombielike look on her face, then all of a sudden she leaned over and stuck her head under the faucet. The water hit her face and sprayed everywhere, soaking the walls, the floor, and me.

"Hey, what's the big idea?" I cried. She didn't budge. Her eyes were closed and her arms were hanging limp at her sides. "Get up or I'll turn the hair dryer on you!" I shouted. That was mean, I know, but I was desperate.

Ariel opened her eyes and stood up. I reached over and turned off the water. She stared at me hard, as if she were trying to look inside my brain. Then she sighed. "You cannot understand."

"You got that right," I said, tossing towels on the wet floor. "Pick out a blouse. I'll be out back."

When I walked outside, I found Cos and Gnarly wrestling on the grass like a couple of puppies. Every time Gnarly barked, Cos barked back. Ariel appeared a moment later, wearing my brand-new white sweater, the one I hadn't even worn yet. Believe it or not, she'd put it on over her own sweater.

Cos stood up and exchanged a glance with my mother. I prayed he and his bizarro daughter were getting ready to leave. Instead, he sat down on the picnic bench and put his arm around Mom.

I frowned. Mom never let her dates get all touchy-feely with her, at least not in front of Mickey and me. I waited for her to move away. She didn't.

"Kids," she said instead, "Cos and I have something to tell you."

He cleared his throat. "I know our families are from different worlds," he began, "and we haven't known each other long. And I know this evening hasn't gone quite as smoothly as we hoped..."

That's an understatement, I thought.

But Mom only smiled and said, "When two people feel the way we do about each other..." She shrugged. "Well, if we follow our hearts, everything's bound to work out. That's why we're..." She turned to Cos.

He grinned and squeezed my mother like a tube of toothpaste. "Congratulate us, kids," he bellowed. "We're engaged!"

FOUR

Ariel's Diary

I am writing this inside our new living box in the region known as Playa Vista. Daddy has brought me here because he intends to commit himself to the Earth woman known as Kathy Larsen.

Oh, horror! Oh, misery! Oh, contemptible fate! And to add to the agony, I have learned that his commitment implies his intent to become the secondary parental figure—stepfather, says my dictionary—of the Earth children Megan and Mickey. And I, without my consent, will become their stepsister.

Oh, vile alien youth. The smaller of the two is loud and brash, constantly chattering and squirming. His actions are unsophisticated, but what of his brain? My father tells me the boy asked if we were from outer space. Does he know the truth? I cannot perceive his thoughts, so I must ask him in words. But is that safe?

The larger youth frightens me even more. She saw

me ingesting helium, which is not a human custom. Fortunately, she seemed to have accepted it. But later, when I viewed her photographs of the activity known as surfing, I became overwhelmed with longing for my home. Desperate to attain a liquid state, I plunged my head into the sink. The girl was startled, I know. Still, her threat to create wind was vicious beyond my understanding.

My thoughts return to the Earth woman. I recoil at the notion of my father sharing his thoughts, feelings, perceptions (these simple words cannot begin to convey what the Zircalonian mind contains) with a mere human being. But of course the intimacies my father and this Earth female share can never be like the ones my mother and father shared on Z-6. No one on Earth can telepathically perceive another's thoughts. Therefore, their knowledge of each other must be shallow. They cannot truly know each other.

I must accept this human deficiency. After all, here on Earth, I cannot perceive thoughts either. Except... the animal they call Gnarly. How flummoxed I was to realize I could perceive his thoughts. And how disappointed. The beast has a brain the size of a helium molecule.

Even worse, I fear the creature has some sort of attraction toward me. Could it be he perceived my thoughts, too? But no, then he would have realized instantly that I was repulsed by his random motions, his hairiness, his loud and loathsome bark. And yet how can I explain the way he bounded into my lap when my father and the Earthling announced their engagement, and the eagerness with which he moistened my face with his tongue?

I paused to converse with my father. I feel a new and foreign emotion when I realize he cannot perceive my thoughts yet. Despite the fact that I daily read my dictionary and thesaurus (a much more pleasurable experience for me than watching television, my father's preferred method of learning English), I haven't been able to find a word for this emotion.

Furthermore, each day I grow more eager to create words on these pages. Not because writing has grown any more satisfying to me; it shall forever remain a pale and pathetic imitation of thought. No, what attracts me is that my father does not read these pages. Cannot read them, for I have been hiding them under the woolly floor covering—the rug—in my sleeping room.

And so I write what is in my mind, knowing full well my father wishes me to feel otherwise. And do otherwise. Yesterday, when he was visiting Kathy Larsen at her store, I took a bus to the self-storage warehouse where Daddy has hidden our disassembled space transport vehicle. (My father built this vehicle from true solids found on GrRp. Alas, if only we'd traveled the Zircalonian way, with Z-6ers taking on temporal solid forms, I would have companions with me now.)

Inside the craft, I found our ComBox, which I brought back to the apartment in order to contact my beloved Zircalonian soul mate, Ffffoopp. Of course, since Earth and Z-6 are many galaxies apart, I could not use the ComBox to transmit and receive brain waves—a moot point since I can no longer perceive thoughts anyway. Instead, I contacted and communicated with Ffffoopp by stimulating the ComBox's concept circuits. The process is a bit like electronic writing, except instead of using cumbersome words and sentences as Earthlings do, the concept circuits transmit entire thoughts.

Naturally, the complexity of our communication cannot be adequately translated into words. Still, I feel a mysterious need to simplify our thoughts into human symbols, to see our words on paper, to remember.

Ffffoopp: Ssweezle, where are you? It's been fourteen moons since you last commed me.

Me: I am on Earth, in the Nebula galaxy, beyond GrRp.

Ffffoopp: But why? You didn't com me that the HEC was sending you there.

Me: They didn't. My father simply wanted to visit. He saw the television transmissions from this planet and was greatly intrigued.

Ffffoopp: He always was strange. Is the environment adequate?

(I transmitted a few representative descriptions of Earth, leaving out the information that I could no longer change form or perceive thoughts. To admit I had devolved so far was just too embarrassing.)

Ffffoopp: Yuck. Is there helium there?

Me: Yes.

Ffffoopp: Then the HEC will be pleased. When do you return?

(Something told me not to share my thoughts. No one has ever left Zircalon-6 permanently, at least not as far as I know. I wasn't sure how Ffffoopp would respond to the news.)

Me: That is unknown.

Ffffoopp: I went to TubeWorld with Turrkel last moon. (He transmitted descriptions of the two of them in a liquid state, splashing together.)

Me: Why Turrkel? She cannot perceive you as I can.

Ffffoopp: It is true, Ssweezle. But I am lonely.

Me: I, too.

Then the salt water flowed from my eyes, and I was glad the ComBox did not have a view screen. I could not bear for Ffffoopp to see me inhabiting a human body. He would be repulsed.

Suddenly, I heard Daddy opening the front door. I quickly signed off and hid the ComBox under my bed. My father soon appeared carrying a sweatshirt with the words PLAYA VISTA MIDDLE SCHOOL on it, a folder of papers, and a pink machine called a bicycle.

And so my life plummets from misery to despair, for my father says I must attend Earth school. Although I am ninety-nine Earth years on Zircalon-6, I inhabit the body of a twelve-year-old here. This means I am to attend a thing known as middle school, at the sixth-grade level. The same classification as the horrid, the cruel, the fearful Megan Larsen.

Tomorrow we ride to school together.

FIVE

As soon as Cos and Ariel left, I confronted my mother. "Have you lost your mind?" I cried. "You can't marry that guy. He's too weird!"

"I like him," my little brother said, turning to Mom, who was loading plates into the dishwasher. "When he moves in, can he share my room?"

"Mickey, don't you get it?" I said. "This dude is going to be our new father."

"Stepfather," Mom corrected. "You already have a father. Cos would never try to replace him."

"Whatever," I said. "The point is, after the wedding Cos and his freaky daughter are going to move in with us. They're going to eat our food, use our bathroom, meet our friends."

"We're not getting married tomorrow," Mom said. "We haven't even set a date. First we want both families to spend time together. We can't become a family until we become friends."

"If you think I'm going to become friends with Ariel, you're nuts," I said.

"I think she's pretty," Mickey announced.

"She's stuck up," I told him. "Did you see the way she looked down her nose at Mom's cooking? And the way she threw a hissy fit about Gnarly?"

"Maybe she's just having a hard time adjusting to life in California," Mom suggested, turning on the dishwasher. "She's a long way from northern Canada. She's probably homesick."

Mom walked into the living room and popped a surfing video into the VCR. Then she grabbed the surfboard propped up in the corner—her "couch potato board." She laid the nose on the coffee table and the tail on the sofa (the fin fit between the cushions) and jumped on.

"I just don't get what you see in that guy," I insisted, flopping down on the sofa beside her board. "He wears a Bugs Bunny sweatshirt and acts like pickles are some kind of delicacy. He's bizarre!"

"Oh, and I guess we're your typical all-American family," Mom replied.

I looked up at her. She was standing on a surfboard in the middle of the living room, "surfing" along with the television. Every time the surfer on the video did a cutback, Mom pretended to do one, too. Mickey walked in wearing an E.T. mask. "Greetings, Earthlings," he said in a squeaky voice.

"Hi, E.T.," Mom said with a wave. The surfer on the video wiped out. Mom tumbled off her board and bounced onto the sofa cushions.

I let out a sigh. Okay, so maybe we weren't the

Brady Bunch. But Cos and Ariel were a lot weirder.

"I know things are happening fast, Meg," Mom said. "I didn't plan on falling in love with anybody. But there's just something about Cos—his enthusiasm for life, his down-to-earth attitude, his laughing green eyes..." Her voice trailed off and she shrugged. "Who can explain love at first sight? I'm head over heels."

"But what about us?" I demanded. "Don't Mickey and I get a say in what happens?"

"I'm sorry," Mom said, squeezing my hand. "I'm probably not handling this very well. I just figured since I adore Cos so much that you would, too."

She turned to Mickey and motioned for him to join us. "Kids, listen to me. If you truly feel you can't accept Cos as your stepfather, I won't marry him. But you have to give him a chance. Ariel, too. I want you both to promise you'll make an effort to get to know them."

"Okay," Mickey said agreeably.

Mom waited for my answer. What could I say? I loved my mother and wanted her to be happy. Besides, if Cos made Mom feel anything like the way Cutter made me feel...well, how could I say no to that? Still, accepting Cos wasn't going to be easy. And as for Ariel...

I pictured her cowering under the coffee table, sucking balloons, sticking her head under the faucet, wrinkling her pert little nose. Let's be honest: It was going to be impossible.

* * *

One week later, Cos and Ariel were living in a rented condo about a mile from our house. Cos hadn't had much luck with his job hunting, so Mom hired him to work at High Tide Ocean Sports, helping her stock the shelves and work the cash register.

As if that weren't bad enough, Ariel was enrolling in my school. Even worse, Mom made me promise to help her find her way around.

"Don't they have *bikes* in northern Canada?" I asked, pedaling beside Ariel as she wobbled down the street on her first day of school. Her bike was pink with babyish handlebar streamers.

"Errr...I'm out of practice," she mumbled.

As we headed into the school parking lot, I noticed kids looking at us. I figured they were thinking, *Who's the dweeb with Megan?* But to my surprise, three boys walked over to us before we'd even locked up our bikes.

"Hi, Megan," Drew Belzer said. "Who's your friend?"

"This is Ariel Cola," I replied, shooting him a look that told him that this girl was not fit to be anyone's friend, let alone mine. But it seemed Drew didn't pick up my signal.

"Hey, Ariel," he said with a grin. "How do you and Megan know each other?"

"Our parents are, uh, friends," I said before Ariel could open her mouth. No way was I going to let anyone know we might become stepsisters. I decided to change the subject. "Ariel's from Canada."

"What was it like up there in the frozen North?" Michael Olhousen asked.

"Uh...frozen," Ariel said in her musical voice. The boys laughed as if she'd actually said something witty.

"You must be a good skier," Skip Harris said.

"I...um...like water," Ariel said, tossing her blond hair. The first bell rang. "What's that?" She looked around uncertainly.

"You didn't have bells at your school?" I asked. "Where did you go—a one-room schoolhouse?"

She gazed above my head. "Yes."

"No kidding," Drew said as if he'd never heard anything so fascinating.

"See you at lunch, Ariel," Michael said. He started jogging up the front steps, then turned and called, "Welcome to Playa Vista Middle School!"

At first I didn't get it. Ariel's conversation was about as interesting as watching glue harden. So why were the boys acting as if she were Ms. Congeniality?

"Because she's drop-dead gorgeous, you idiot," Tara whispered when I asked her. Tara, Robin, and I were at our lockers, putting away our jackets.

Naturally, my two best friends had already heard plenty from me about Cos and Ariel, but this was the first time they'd actually seen my potential stepsister.

I glanced across the hall to where Ariel was fiddling with her new combination lock. Yep, she was beautiful all right. I'd been so busy hating her personality that I'd almost forgotten.

"I wouldn't want to have *her* for a stepsister," Tara said. "I'd feel so inferior."

"Inferior to her?" I laughed. "She's got the personality of a jellyfish."

"Yeah, but you know boys," Robin said. "When it comes to girls, all they want is a pretty package. They don't really care what's inside."

Is Cutter like that? I wondered. I couldn't believe it. After all, I wasn't anything special to look at— brown hair, brown eyes, a nothing-to-write-home-about body—but he still liked me. Or at least, I hoped he did.

"Here she comes," Robin whispered, tilting her head in the direction of Ariel, who was doing her cloud imitation.

"Why are you still wearing your jacket?" I asked her as she floated to a stop in front of me.

"It's cold," she said, gazing at that now-familiar spot over my head.

Just then, the second bell rang. "Uh-oh." I took off running with Tara and Robin beside me. The three of us were halfway down the hall before I realized Ariel wasn't with us. I looked over my shoulder to find her drifting along in slow motion.

"Hurry up," I called. "We're going to be late."

Her response was to accelerate from a snail's pace to the speed of cold molasses.

Forget her, I told myself. *Let her fend for herself.*

But then I remembered the promise I'd made my mother to help her out—and my bigger promise to get to know her.

With a groan, I forced myself to stop and wait.

We were late to homeroom, of course, and Mr. Braggle made me write THE EARLY BIRD CATCHES THE WORM on the blackboard fifty times. However, since Ariel was new to the school, he forgave her. Then he asked her to tell the class about her hometown.

"It's small," she said in a near whisper. "Remote. Very quiet. Errr...can I use the rest room?"

Hmm, I thought, *maybe Mom was right when she said Ariel was shy.* But I changed my mind when I saw her between classes. She was surrounded by boys, all jostling to get near her, and I could tell she was loving it. I mean, she was still acting aloof, but if you asked me, she wasn't feeling shy. She was playing hard to get.

Our first subject was math. The teacher, Mrs. Hayvenhurst, didn't believe in waiting for students to raise their hands. She just called on you. And when she called on Ariel, she got a surprise.

"Ariel, can you calculate the volume of this swimming pool?" Mrs. Hayvenhurst pointed to the shape on the blackboard.

"I assume you wish me to visualize the trapezoidal side as the base?" Ariel asked.

"Oh, wait, I drew that incorrectly," Mrs. Hayvenhurst said, reaching for the eraser. "We haven't studied trapezoids yet. That's supposed to be a rectangle."

"The trapezoidal base has an area of $1/2$ x (8 + 3) x 40, equaling 220 square feet," Ariel said. Then she solved the rest of the problem.

Jeez, what an egghead! *One more reason I don't want Ariel as a stepsister,* I thought. I mean, the last thing I needed was some brain around the house for Mom to compare me to.

Ariel kept her mouth shut during English and social studies, so I couldn't tell if she was a whiz in those subjects, too. Then, finally, lunchtime rolled around. We had barely walked into the cafeteria when Heather Harper, one of the prettiest and most popular girls in the school (and the girlfriend of Raleigh Easton, a Stingray), asked Ariel to sit with her. Ariel accepted, completely ignoring Tara, Robin, and me. Not that I wanted her to eat lunch with me (if you could call it eating—all she did was lick a few blobs of yogurt off a spoon). Still, I figured she owed me after the way I'd stuck by her all morning.

When the bell rang, Heather appeared at my shoulder. "Hi, Megan," she said sweetly. I was so surprised I couldn't speak. Heather had never so much as looked at me before.

"Ariel told me you two are going to be step-sisters," she chirped. "You must be so excited."

I frowned. Why did Ariel have to tell everyone that? "It's not a sure thing," I said. "Our parents are just dating, that's all."

"Ariel's different from anyone I've ever met,"

Heather said. "She's so together, so deep—sort of mysterious. And I'm dying to know what kind of conditioner she uses on her hair. Do you know?"

"Not really."

"Well, anyway," Heather continued. "Everyone knows that the Stingrays hang out at Pelican Point after school. Why don't you come by and join us sometime—with Ariel, of course." Without waiting for my reply, she hurried off to join her friends.

Tara and Robin had been listening from the other side of the table. Now they let out an ecstatic shriek. "An invitation from Heather Harper to hang out with the Stingrays!" Tara squealed. "Wow!"

"Can we come along?" Robin asked. "Please?"

"I'm not going," I said, pushing my chair back.

"What?" Tara cried. "Why not?"

"Look, it was bad enough having Ariel over at my house. Now it turns out I'm going to have to see her in school every day. If you think I'm going to spend my spare time with her, too, you're dead wrong."

"Megan Larsen, you are so selfish!" Robin cried.

"Yeah," Tara agreed. "Ariel isn't so bad. She's a little odd, but Heather likes her, right?"

Just then, Ariel walked by, surrounded by boys. As usual, she was gazing off into space. Tara and Robin jumped up from their seats.

"Ariel, wait up," Tara called, hurrying after her.

"Come on, Megan," Robin called before following Tara through the cafeteria door with the rest of the Ariel fan club.

I sat there, too stunned to move. When I'd first told Tara and Robin about my potential weirdo stepsister, they'd been sympathetic. Now they were falling all over themselves to get near her.

"Hey, Megan," a familiar voice called. I turned to find Cutter standing behind me. Suddenly, all my troubles seemed to sprout wings and fly away.

"Hi, Cutter," I said. "What's up?"

"Did you see that new girl Ariel?" he asked.

My heart dropped like a lead sinker. "Uh, yeah," I muttered, pointing to the door. "She went that way."

"Thanks, Megan. See you at the beach." With that, he turned and practically sprinted out the door.

SIX

Ariel's Diary

I do not understand Earth boys. For some unknown reason, they desire to speak with me, but their conversation is pathetically empty and meaningless. Furthermore, they seem to delight in my every word, no matter how hesitant or uninformed.

I have tried to avoid them—even to ignore them— but they follow me about, calling my name and inviting me to partake of various foods (yech) and social activities with them. Are they treating me kindly because it is an Earth custom to welcome newcomers? Or are they investigating me because they suspect I am not one of their own?

I asked my father, who told me that Earth males find my solid human body beautiful. I am certain Daddy is misinformed, however, for I look no different from the other Earth girls in my age group. Like them, I have the normal female characteristics, including a soprano speaking voice and a minimum of body hair. The only thing unusual about my physical form is my eyes, which are more purple than those of most Earthlings I've observed thus far. But surely that does not make me more visually pleasing than others.

Now, sitting alone in my room, I remember my first day at school with despair. The disciplines they call math and science are based on logic and principles that are familiar to me and do not tax my mind. But the subjects of literature and social studies perplex me. They concern the behavior of humanity, while I still cannot even comprehend the actions of the humans who stand before me.

For example, today a girl named Heather invited me to the ocean. Since viewing the photos of Kathy Larsen surfing, I have been eager to observe human ocean-related activities, and I wanted to tell Heather yes.

But when I asked Megan to accompany Heather and me to the beach, she scowled. "You're Miss Popularity, aren't you?" she asked.

"I don't know," I said. "Am I?"

"Go with your new friends" was her only reply. "You don't need me."

Why was Megan angry? And why does she perceive I do not need her? In truth, I long for someone who understands my Zircalonian soul, someone who can help me to survive on this alien planet, someone who cares. I look to my father, but he is like a youth experiencing his liquid state for the first time. His senses are so befuddled that he can think only of himself and his newfound joy. He has no time for me.

*   *   *

The sun has risen once more and I write of good news. I have found a friend! True, she is a human being, but she has many harmonious character traits.

Her name is Serena Soo, and she is the superintendent of the condominium complex in which we reside. I met her last night when Daddy sent me to deliver our rent check. As I bent down to slip the check through the mail slot, the door opened and there she was—a tall, willowy human with long black hair and a quiet grace. She smiled, asked my name, and invited me inside. As she walked, her pink, loose-fitting garment flowed around her legs, reminding me most pleasingly of my gaseous soul mates on Z-6.

After exchanging the normal human pleasantries, Serena informed me that she is a psychic and fortune-teller. This, she explained, means she can perceive the thoughts of other human beings and predict the future. Imagine my excitement at finding an Earthling who can perceive my thoughts! Perhaps, I told myself, she can teach me to regain my own powers of perception.

Alas, I soon discovered that although Serena seems sincere, she is mistaken about her abilities. I know this because when I concentrated hard on the thought that there was an enormous man with a knife climbing in the window behind her, she did not show any signs of alarm or even curiosity.

Nonetheless, Serena is perceptive, for a human. She sensed at once that I was not from Playa Vista and that I felt out of place. She guessed also that I was at odds with my father, and that I longed to return to my place of birth. What's more, she told me that she felt confident that I, too, have psychic powers but that something is inhibiting them.

Of course, I could not tell Serena the whole truth, but I did say that before I moved to California, I had possessed the ability to perceive minds. Serena became excited and suggested I might regain my powers through something called meditation and crystal healing. She even promised to help. In return, she asked for a mere ten dollars per session—to cover the cost of the crystals.

Naturally, I agreed. I don't have the money, but I believe my father will give it to me. Despite his apparent cheer, I feel certain that he, too, longs to perceive other minds once again, especially mine.

Oh, woe! Oh, misery! Disaster has struck.

It happened this afternoon. My joy at meeting Serena was so great that I longed to share the news with Ffffoopp. So, when school let out, I rushed home and took the ComBox from under my bed. But, to my sorrow, my beloved did not want to speak of Earth. His only interest was in knowing how soon I would return home. When I did not answer, he sent me random images of himself at TubeWorld making waves with Turrkel.

Me: Why do you choose to splash with Turrkel?

Ffffoopp: She perceives me well. And her father has a great mind. He is working on a way to repair Zircalonian molecules scattered by the wind.

(How could I respond? My father is a mere underling for the HEC. In fact, he is no longer even that respectable. He has turned his back on Zircalon-6 and everything it stands for. He is a...I must check my thesaurus...a *defector*.)

Me: Ffffoopp, I want to share something—

At that moment, my father arrived home and walked into my room. He took one look at the ComBox and stopped short. Then he grabbed it and quickly terminated my transmission.

"Who were you communicating with?" he demanded.

"Ffffoopp," I said.

"Don't you realize how dangerous that is? What if he tells the Governing Council?"

"Who cares?" I replied, my eyes flowing with water. "They're probably happy to get rid of you. You're not a normal Zircalonian. You're strange!"

My father flinched at my harsh words but did not respond directly to them. Instead, he told me, "In the Helium Exploration Corps, there was once a lone Zircalonian who left Z-6. The Governing Council sent the HEC to bring him back. He spent the rest of his life as a lug nut."

I cringed. Imagine being forced to spend one's entire life in the shape of a common lug nut. It is a cruel enough fate to be solid here on Earth, where solidity is the norm. But to live solid on Z-6? What humiliation! What disgrace! I would not wish such a fate on my father. I would not wish it on anyone.

"Ffffoopp would never betray me," I said. "Besides, I told him we will return home soon."

I felt my cheeks grow hot. Daddy did not realize that at the moment he came into the room, I had been about to tell Ffffoopp the truth of our new life. Once again I felt that unfamiliar emotion, which thus far has no name. And once again I longed to return to Z-6, where emotions are easily understood and gloriously serene.

"Daddy," I said, eager to change the subject, "I have pleasing news. I have met a woman who says she can help us regain our ability to perceive minds. All she asks in return is ten dollars per session."

My father frowned. "I don't want to perceive others' thoughts. It's not a human ability."

"But you are not human!" I cried. "You are a Zircalonian, and so am I. We do not belong on this planet."

Daddy leaned over and touched my face—an Earth gesture of tenderness that felt especially foreign coming from one of my own.

"We're not going back," he said quietly. "We can't. For better or worse, we are Earthlings now."

SEVEN

By the end of Ariel's first week at school, I never wanted to hear her name again. The entire school was talking about the girl—her beauty, her grace, her talent in math and science, her mysterious personality. And, of course, since Ariel was my potential stepsister, everyone assumed I must know all about her.

Did she have a boyfriend? My classmates wanted to know. Had I ever visited her hometown? Did she like rap music? What was her favorite color? As if I knew. Or cared.

At first I simply acted uninterested. "Ariel and I aren't very close," I told everyone.

"You aren't?" the kids would ask incredulously, as if I were passing up a chance to hobnob with Princess Di or something.

I finally lost it on Friday when Cutter Colburne asked me why Ariel and I hadn't shown up at Pelican Point to hang out with the Stingrays. Instead of shrugging off his question, I snapped out what I was really thinking. "Because I'd rather eat dirt than spend two minutes with Ariel Cola."

"But I thought you two were friends," Cutter said with surprise.

"It would be easier to befriend an ice cube," I said, secretly hoping he'd thank me for enlightening him.

Instead, he frowned and said, "That's kind of harsh, Megan." Then he walked away.

Great. So now the entire school—including my two best friends and the boy of my dreams—thought Ariel was the greatest thing since pop-top cans. And that I was a moron for not agreeing with them.

That evening, Mom announced that she and Cos were going out to dinner and a movie—and that Ariel was coming over to help me baby-sit Mickey.

"But why?" I cried. "I baby-sit Mickey all the time. I don't need her help."

"I want you three to spend some time together," Mom replied.

"Oh, boy!" Mickey exclaimed as Mom went into her bedroom to change. "Maybe Ariel will tell me a bedtime story about her travels in outer space!"

"Earth to Mickey," I called. "Ariel is not from outer space. The only alien planet she's ever visited is the planet Weird."

"Oh, yeah?" he challenged. "Have you noticed she and Cos never go to the bathroom? They're not like us."

Just then, the doorbell rang. Mom opened the

door and there was Cos wearing some kind of strange-looking yellow and red kimono thing and carrying a bunch of helium-filled balloons. Ariel appeared behind him, wafting along in her own personal fog bank.

"There's frozen pizza in the freezer," Mom said. "I wrote down the phone numbers of where we'll be."

"Have fun, kids," Cos called, heading out.

As they drove away, Ariel walked over to the sofa and sat down primly. "I need to do my homework," she said, opening a canvas bag and pulling out her schoolbooks. One by one, she gingerly picked up the papers that were strewn across the coffee table and set them on the floor.

"Don't worry," I said sarcastically. "The rats and cockroaches only come out at night."

"What do you mean?" she asked.

"I mean, you don't have to act as if everything you touch in our house is crawling with germs. We do clean once in a while, you know."

"It is not disease-producing microorganisms that trouble me," she explained. "You have too many objects. My mind attempts to organize and categorize them, but I cannot."

"Oh, and I suppose your place looks like something out of *House Beautiful*?"

"Back home we had no use for superfluous solid objects," she said. She opened her social studies book and began reading.

I turned to exchange a look with Mickey, but he

was heading down the hallway toward his room.

"Hey, Ariel," I said, sitting down on the sofa next to her, "you wouldn't just happen to have your math homework with you, would you? Maybe I could just check my answers against—"

"It would be improper to allow you to copy my homework," she said.

"Who said anything about copying?" I demanded. "I just need a little help. In return, I could give you a hand with your social studies homework."

"Each student must do his or her own work," Ariel said in a prissy little voice.

"Oh, excuse me," I replied, jumping to my feet. "I didn't know I was talking to Mother Teresa."

"Who is that?"

"Stop acting like you grew up in another solar system," I said. "Northern Canada isn't in outer space, you know."

"Of course not," she replied. "It is on planet Earth, in the Northern Hemisphere."

"Give it a rest, Ariel," I snapped. "This mysterious I-am-not-of-this-world act you've been putting on doesn't impress me. I know you're just doing it to keep the boys interested in you. But there's one boy you'd better keep away from. Cutter Colburne is mine, and don't you forget it."

"I have no interest in Cutter Colburne or any other boy," Ariel said, sweeping back her long blond hair. "I have a soul mate of my own back home."

Talk about good news! For the first time since I'd

met Ariel, I felt like hugging her. "No kidding," I said. "What's his name?"

"It is...er...uh...it's a secret."

"A secret? Why? Is he famous or something?"

"No. He's just, er...special, that's all. And very different from the boys around here. More intelligent, more perceptive, more–"

I cut her off. "You know, just because you're beautiful doesn't mean you have to act so stuck up."

"I am not beautiful." She looked down at herself and wrinkled her tiny nose. "I am repulsive."

"Oh, pu-*leeze!*" I cried. "Don't give me that false-modesty stuff. You're gorgeous and you know it."

I had barely gotten the last word out of my mouth when Mickey came running into the living room. He was wearing his silver astronaut uniform and holding a purple plastic space gun.

"Ariel," he began eagerly, "next time you go on a trip into outer space, can I go, too?"

Mickey looked so silly, it was all I could do to keep from laughing. But Ariel took one look at him and threw herself to the floor.

"Do not blow wind!" she wailed, cowering against the sofa. "Have mercy on my molecules!"

"This isn't a hair dryer," Mickey said. "It's a ray gun. See?" He pulled the trigger. The multicolored lights on the barrel flashed as the gun whined.

Ariel let out a bloodcurdling shriek and leaped behind the sofa.

I shook my head in astonishment. "Get a grip, Ariel," I called over the back of the couch. "Mickey's not going to hurt you. He's just playing."

Mickey joined me on the sofa, and we both peered down at her. "It's just pretend," he said, thrusting the gun toward her. "You wanna try it?"

Ariel whimpered and tried to squeeze her entire body under the sofa. "Oh for goodness' sake, get up!" I shouted. I reached down, grabbed the back of her collar and pulled. Ariel staggered to her knees, then burst into tears.

"Why are you being so cruel to me?" she sobbed. "I am trying to understand your ways, but I cannot perceive why you threaten me with a weapon."

"And we can't *perceive* why the heck you're so bent out of shape by a stupid toy gun," I shot back.

"It is not simply the gun," she sniffed. "It is everything—the strange people, the solid objects, the bizarre customs. I was barely beginning to comprehend the structure of your society when my father announced that he was marrying your mother and we were to become a family. Oh, dread! Oh, horrid agony!" she wailed. "I wish I were dead!"

I stared at her, barely able to believe my ears. "You don't want your father to marry our mother?"

"I would rather have my molecules separated in a windstorm!" she cried passionately.

A grin crept across my cheeks. "This is great news."

"Why?" she asked, blinking back tears.

"Because I feel exactly the same way."

Mickey shook his head. "I don't. I—"

"It's past your bedtime," I broke in.

"It is not. It's barely dinnertime."

"I'll make you a deal," I said, grabbing his arm and dragging him into the kitchen. There was an idea brewing inside my head and I wanted Mick out of the way. "If you get ready for bed right now, you can eat cookies for dinner. Plus, you can watch *E.T.* on the VCR in Mom's bedroom."

His face lit up. "Cool!" He grabbed a box of chocolate cookies and disappeared down the hall.

"Ariel," I said, striding back into the living room, "I think we can stop this wedding. But we've got to join forces and work together."

She eyed me suspiciously, probably wondering how she could work with someone she disliked so much. Actually, I felt exactly the same way. In fact, I was starting to have second thoughts. Could the two of us put aside our feelings long enough to pull off the scheme I had in mind?

I opened my mouth, all set to call off the whole thing, when Ariel said softly, "If you have devised a method for halting our parents' plan to wed, I am interested."

I hesitated, wondering if I had made a big mistake.

"And Megan," Ariel continued, "if you help me with my social studies homework, I will assist you with your mathematics equations."

Suddenly, I was feeling much warmer toward Ariel. Maybe we *could* work together after all. At least, I was willing to try. I sat down on the sofa and motioned for her to join me. "Let's do it," I said with a smile.

EIGHT

Ariel's Diary

I have discovered the name of the strange emotion I have been experiencing of late. According to Megan Larsen, it is called "guilt."

She, however, does not seem hindered by it. When she explained that her plan for deterring the wedding involves tricking our parents into becoming angry with each other, I was dismayed. I expressed concern, but Megan said the plan is for a good cause and is therefore justified.

Is she right?

I tell myself yes. After all, my father was born a Zircalonian. To live as an Earthling, to marry and become the stepfather of Earth children—surely that is wrong. I must guide my father, even if it involves a measure of deceit.

But are my actions motivated by my own selfish desires? I have not adapted to life on this planet. I long to return to my home, my gaseous existence, my soul mate Ffffoopp. That is my dream, my desire.

But what of my father's dreams and desires? Do I dare destroy his happiness in order to regain my own?

Yet another anxiety overcomes me: What if Megan's plan works and my father's attraction to Kathy is deleted? Does that mean he will return to Z-6? Or will he remain on Earth and commit to another woman? At least Kathy Larsen has a kind smile, a soothing voice, and an affinity for water. Who knows what sort of horrid Earthling my father might choose next—and what sort of repugnant children might come with her?

More and more I feel the need to communicate with Ffffoopp. Since my father removed the ComBox I have tried to forget him and foster my friendship with Serena. Of course, Daddy would not give me the money for our sessions, but I have stopped buying lunch at school (no sacrifice there) and am using that money to pay her.

Although my ability to perceive minds has not yet returned, I find pleasure in my sessions with Serena. Meditation is pleasant, and quite similar to Zircalonian reflection. The crystal healing, which mostly involves Serena dangling lumps of glass over my body, does not seem very helpful. But, after a long day at school, I do enjoy the calm of her home.

Still, it is not the same as sharing my thoughts with Ffffoopp. Shall I disobey my father, locate the ComBox, and contact him? Once again I am awash in the strange feeling called guilt. Oh, this Earthly life is confusing! I must inhale helium and think.

*　　　*　　　*

Ffffoopp knows everything!

I found the ComBox under the pile of dirty laundry beneath my father's bed. When Daddy went out, I contacted Ffffoopp.

Of course, he was appalled to learn that my father has elected to remain on Earth forever. Furthermore, he approves of Megan's plan. He says that whatever it takes to get my father and me off this planet and back to Z-6, I must do it.

Lying, trickery, deceit, and their accompanying emotion, guilt—while never condoned on Z-6—are justified in this case because my father has clearly taken leave of his senses. That is what Ffffoopp perceives, and I know he must be right. He has a nimble mind, a deep understanding of Zircalonian interpersonal relations, and a glorious gaseousness, which is surpassed only by his vigorous wetness.

And yet I pause to think how odd it is that my beloved Ffffoopp perceives life the same—at least in this case—as my least favorite Earth creature, Megan Larsen. If Ffffoopp and Megan can approach a problem with parallel reasoning, is it perhaps possible that Megan and I could someday grow to comprehend and respect each other?

This is a concept that confounds even my expansive Zircalonian mind. But no matter. Soon (if our plan succeeds and Daddy elects to return to Z-6) Megan, Mickey, Kathy Larsen, and their vile, hairy canine will be nothing but a distant and distasteful memory.

NINE

"Hey, Mom," I said, plopping down on her bed the next morning, "guess what Ariel told me last night."

Mom opened one sleepy eye. "What are you doing up so early?"

"I don't know. I was just thinking about what a good time Ariel and I had last night, that's all."

Mom opened both eyes. "You had a good time?"

I nodded. "We helped each other with our homework, ate some ice cream. It was fun."

I wasn't lying. What I didn't mention was that we'd also devised a plan to transform our parents from lovesick puppies into snarling tigers.

"See?" Mom said, suddenly all smiles. "I knew there was more to Ariel than met the eye. You just had to break through her shyness, right?"

Right, I thought, there was more to Ariel than met the eye. Like, for example, she drank about five glasses of water in an hour and never once went to the bathroom. Plus, the only thing she ate all night was one piece of pepperoni off her pizza.

No wonder Mickey thought she was an alien. But I knew better. If you asked me, that girl had an eating disorder. It was just a matter of time before she ended up in some rehab clinic with a tube up her nose.

"So we were talking about you and Cos," I said innocently, "and Ariel told me a secret about her dad."

"What is it?" Mom asked eagerly.

"Cos thinks you watch too much TV," I lied.

Mom's face fell. "But Cos watches TV, too. He has one in his condo. I've seen it."

"Yes, but Ariel says he only watches educational shows. Anyway, he's decided to get rid of it and spend more time at the theater and the symphony."

"Really?" Mom looked puzzled. "Why didn't he tell me he liked the theater and the symphony? We've been going to lots of movies. I thought he loved them."

"Oh, Ariel says Cos would never want to hurt your feelings. He thinks you're so much fun. The words she said he used were 'refreshingly simple.'"

"Simple?" Mom repeated with a frown. "It sounds as if he thinks I'm stupid."

"Oh, no," I said quickly. "Ariel says her father thinks you're very intelligent—for a California girl."

Mom looked hurt. "I may not be an intellectual, but I'm not dumb. I'm more the outdoor type, that's all. I thought Cos liked that about me."

I shrugged. "I'm just reporting what I heard."

* * *

Mom spent the morning moping around the house. Whenever I walked into the living room, she was staring off into space and frowning. Finally, at lunchtime, she announced she was going out.

An hour later, she returned with five CDs of classical music, an assortment of novels, and *The Complete Shakespeare.* Then she put our television in a plastic garbage bag and took it to the garage.

When Cos came over later, armed with his usual bouquet of balloons, I was in the kitchen. From behind the door, I secretly watched everything going on in the living room.

"Hi, Kathy," Cos boomed, pulling her into a crushing bear hug. "I've got a surprise for you!"

"I've got a surprise for you, too."

Cos glanced at the empty space where our television used to be. "What happened to the TV?"

"That's the surprise," Mom announced. "I got rid of it."

Cos was surprised, all right. In fact, he looked completely floored. "You got rid of it? Why?"

"I was watching too much junk." She walked over to the sofa and held up one of the novels. "From now on, I'm going to spend my spare time studying the great works of music and literature."

"No kidding," Cos said without much enthusiasm. He gazed forlornly at the space where the TV used to be, then turned back to Mom. "Listen, there's a kite festival in Shoreline Park this afternoon—"

"Now, Cos," Mom cut in, "just because I'm a

surfer doesn't mean I have to be out in the sun twenty-four hours a day." She sat on the sofa and patted the cushion beside her. "Come join me."

Cos looked puzzled. "Well, okay, if that's what you want." He let his balloons float to the ceiling.

Cos sat and Mom opened *The Complete Shakespeare*. "Here's a wonderful sonnet I read this morning. Shall I read it to you?"

"Okay," Cos said reluctantly.

Mom began to read. Cos leaned back and stared at the ceiling. After about ten seconds, he jumped onto the coffee table.

Mom stopped reading. "What are you doing?"

"There's a spider on the ceiling," he announced. "I want to get a better look at it."

"But I'm right in the middle of the sonnet."

"Oh, sorry." Cos hopped off the coffee table and sat down. He stretched. "Okay, go ahead."

Mom took a deep breath and went back to reading. Cos began to mutter under his breath.

Mom looked up. "What?"

"I was trying to remember the words to the *Barney and Friends* theme song. How does it go?" He began to sing. "I love you, you love me—"

"Cos," Mom interrupted irritably, "do you or do you not want me to read a sonnet to you?"

"I do not," he said simply.

"But why?"

"Your normal speaking voice is energetic and upbeat," he said, "but when you were reading, it was flat and dull. I think you'd be happier if we went out."

Mom crossed her arms over her chest and frowned. "I don't get it, Cos. If you think I'm such an airhead, why did you ask me to marry you?"

"Because you've got beautiful eyes," he replied with a smile, "and hair the color of sand, and—"

"So that's all I am to you?" Mom cried. "A pretty face? What about my brain?"

"I don't know," Cos said, looking confused. "I've never seen your brain."

Mom stiffened. "That was low. You know, just because you sold your television doesn't mean you're a better person than I am. And if you think it does, you can take your stupid balloons and—"

Just then, the telephone rang. Mom jumped up and grabbed the receiver. "Hello?...Yes..." She frowned. "What? Who told you such a thing?... What?! It's not true. Absolutely not. Good-bye!"

She slammed down the phone. "That was *Surf Scene* magazine. Can you believe it? Someone called and told them I was planning to compete in the Playa Vista Surf Tournament tomorrow after-noon."

"Surprise!" Cos exclaimed. "I know you haven't competed in a surfing contest for years, and I decided it was time you did. So I entered you."

I peeked around the kitchen door and grinned. Everything was going according to plan. Last night, I'd told Ariel to tell her father that Mom missed competitive surfing and was eager to get back on the tour circuit, but she wasn't sure if Cos would approve.

The truth is, although Mom used to be one of the hottest surfers around, she never really liked competing. As far as she's concerned, surfing is about soul, not fame and fortune.

"And don't think the surfing world has forgotten about you," Cos continued, "because when I called *Surf Scene* and told them what was going on, they were very excited. They plan to cover the contest, and interview you, and—"

"What?" Mom gasped. She shook her head. "Oh, Cos, how could you?"

He shrugged. "It's okay, Kath. You don't have to thank me."

"*Thank* you?" Mom cried. "I'm furious with you!"

Cos's mouth fell open. "Furious? But why?"

"Because you're a pompous snob who only likes me for my looks. And because you think I'm a dumb jock whose only goal is to get a surfing trophy."

"Kathy, I'm very disappointed in you," Cos said reproachfully. "I thought you were a kind and gentle woman, but today you resemble a shrill and strident guest on a daytime talk show."

"What do you know about daytime talk shows, Mr. Educational TV?" Mom demanded.

"I know that watching them is more fun than sitting in this musty house listening to your bored voice read a book with small print," Cos replied.

"Then go find someone else to listen to!" Mom

shouted, striding to her bedroom and slamming the door.

"Thank you, I will!" he cried. Then he grabbed his balloons and left.

As soon as Cos was gone, I rushed to the phone and called Ariel. "It worked!" I announced triumphantly. "They just had a huge fight."

"And they ended their commitment to each other?" she asked.

"It sure looks that way."

"I am pleased," Ariel said. "Your plan was a very wise one, Megan."

"Thanks," I replied. "But I couldn't have pulled it off without you."

"Thank you. I will see you in school tomorrow."

"Okay. Bye."

It was only after I'd hung up that I realized Ariel and I had just shared a pleasant conversation. In fact, she'd even given me a compliment. Talk about weird. We'd finally managed to make our parents hate each other, and now we were starting to like—well, at least tolerate—each other.

I stared at the telephone. *Are we doing the right thing?* I wondered. But then I recalled the dreamy look in Cutter's eyes when he'd asked me about Ariel. And I stopped wondering.

TEN

The next day, I woke up to the sound of a man's voice asking, "Where do you want it, lady?"

"Against the wall, right across from the sofa," I heard my mother saying.

I jumped out of bed, threw on my robe, and hurried into the living room just in time to see two deliverymen lowering a big-screen TV to the floor.

"What's going on?" I asked.

Mom let the deliverymen out before she answered. "I was so upset about fighting with Cos that I couldn't sleep. Finally, at three in the morning, I called him." She smiled happily. "We worked things out—and this is my way of saying I'm sorry."

"Gee, that's great," I said, but my heart was sinking.

At that moment the doorbell rang. Mom walked to the door and flung it open. Cos was standing there holding a ragged bouquet of half-wilted weeds and wildflowers, smiling sheepishly. Ariel was behind him, head hung low.

"They're lovely!" Mom said with a laugh.

"I picked them on the way over." He sniffed a dandelion as delicately as if it were a rare orchid.

As Cos handed Mom the flowers, Mickey skipped into the room. "What's with the weeds?" he asked.

Cos responded by falling to his knees. "Can you ever forgive me?" he cried, hugging Mom around the waist.

Mom ruffled Cos's shaggy hair. "I'm the one who needs to apologize. I treated you horribly. But I bought something to make it up to you." She took his hands and pulled him up. "Look."

When Cos spotted the TV, he broke into an ear-to-ear grin. "It's big!" he exclaimed happily.

"It's got stereo sound," Mom said.

"Oh, boy!" Mickey cried. "Let's try it out."

Cos checked his watch. "Yippee! It's almost time for *Sesame Street*."

How about that? It turned out I hadn't lied when I told my mother that Cos liked educational shows. He just preferred the kiddie kind. Somehow, I wasn't surprised.

Mom picked up the remote, but Cos gently took her wrist and pulled her toward him. "Before you turn it on, I want to apologize, too," he said. "I shouldn't have entered you in that surf contest without your permission. But I've got the perfect solution." He turned to me. "Megan, how'd you like to compete in the contest instead of your mom?"

"Me?" I gasped.

Cos nodded. "After the first time we ate dinner at your house, Ariel told me she had seen photographs of you surfing. And your friends Tara and Robin tell me that you're very talented."

I couldn't believe what I was hearing. "You talked to Tara and Robin? About *me?*"

"I didn't want to make the same mistake I made with your mother, so I asked Ariel the names of your closest friends. Then I called them. They told me that you'd like to become a world champion."

"You would?" Mom asked with surprise.

It was true. I did dream of becoming a world-class professional surfer someday. But I'd never told Mom because she didn't approve of surfing for money. Besides, with a name like Larsen, I'd have a lot to live up to. What if I wasn't good enough?

"It's just a fantasy," I said at last. "I'd probably make a fool of myself—and embarrass you."

"Don't be silly, Megan," Mom replied, stepping forward to look me in the eye. "You've got the moves. If you can combine them with hard work and desire, you could go all the way."

"But I thought you hated surf contests," I said.

"I do. That doesn't mean you have to feel the same way. If you want to compete, I'll support you one hundred percent."

"That's good," Cos said, "because I entered Megan in the twelve-to-eighteen-year-old division. She competes today at eleven o'clock."

I was getting more excited by the second. My first

surf contest! "Okay," I said, before I could chicken out. "I'll do it."

"Good for you," Cos said. "And I've got an idea. Let's call back *Surf Scene* magazine and tell them we made a mistake—it isn't Kathy Larsen who's competing today—it's her daughter."

"Let me call," Mom said, grabbing a copy of *Surf Scene* from the coffee table and heading into the kitchen. "I want them to know I'm passing on my crown to a new surfing legend."

"If that isn't worth a feature article, I'll eat a bar of surf wax!" Cos exclaimed.

At that point, I didn't know whether to kiss Cos or strangle him. I was nervous enough about making my contest debut without having an international surfing magazine documenting my every cutback. I mean, what if I got in the water and made a total fool of myself? I could see the headline now: DAUGHTER OF SURF LEGEND PROVES HERSELF A SURF LOSER.

Mom walked out of the kitchen. "They're sending a reporter and a photographer, too," she announced.

"Oh, goody!" Cos exclaimed. "If Megan wins, maybe they'll do a mother-daughter interview."

Jeez, don't put any pressure on me or anything, I thought irritably. But when I looked at Cos's smile, I couldn't be angry. He had done his best to make things right with my mother, and he'd managed to help me out in the process, too. He'd even gone to the trouble of calling up my friends to make sure he was doing the right thing.

"Thanks, Cos," I said. He grabbed me in one of his bear hugs and practically broke my collarbone. As I pulled away, I found myself face to face with my mother, and she didn't look half as happy as Cos.

"Gosh, look at the time!" I exclaimed. "We'd better get down to the beach so I can warm up."

"Not so fast, young lady," Mom said, grabbing my arm. "*Both* young ladies." She glanced at Ariel, who was sitting on the sofa, looking as if she'd like to crawl underneath the cushions. "Ariel, why did you tell Cos I wanted to enter a surf contest?"

"It was a misunderstanding," I piped up. "I told Ariel how much you love to surf and how I want to join the tour, and I guess she got mixed up and thought it was you who wanted to compete."

"You don't say," Mom said skeptically. "And Megan, why did you tell me Cos thought I watched too much TV?"

"Er...that was my fault," Ariel said. "I wanted my father to watch less TV, and I thought if you got rid of your television set, he might do the same. So...er... I told Megan...that is, Megan told me..."

"I don't believe a word of it," Mom said sternly. "I think you two were trying to make us break up."

Suddenly, Ariel burst out crying. "It's true," she wailed. "I have used my father's inability to perceive thoughts for my own selfish purposes. Oh, shame! I have disgraced myself and my people!"

Boy, what a performance. And to think I'd called Ariel aloof and emotionless. When her neck was on the line, she could really turn on the tears. It was working, too. Mom looked really concerned.

"Oh, Ariel, don't cry," she said. "I know it hasn't been easy moving to a new country and starting at a new school. And now you're being asked to accept a whole new family. It's no wonder you stretched the truth a little. You're under so much stress."

Hmmm, I thought to myself, *if it worked for Ariel...*I rubbed my eyes and managed a sniffle. "Everything's happened so fast," I whimpered. "I guess I just couldn't deal with it. I lied, too."

I glanced at Mom. She didn't look impressed. But Cos threw his arm around my shoulders and squeezed me until I thought my chest would explode.

"There, there, Megan," he boomed. "Don't be so hard on yourself."

"Can we go to the beach *now?*" Mickey asked.

"In a minute," Mom said. "Sit down, kids."

We did. *Here it comes,* I thought. *Our punishment.*

"We don't condone what you girls did," Mom said with a frown. Then her expression softened. "But we understand. Cos and I don't expect miracles. We realize it's going to take time for our families to become one. All we ask is that you give each other a chance. Talk to each other, have a little fun—"

"And," Cos broke in, "what better way to have fun than at the beach!" Quickly, he unzipped his pants and let them fall to his ankles, revealing a pair of fluorescent orange swim trunks decorated with yellow and purple surfboards. "What do you say, Megan? Do I look like a real surfer dude?"

Mickey burst out laughing, and Mom joined in. But I gazed at Cos's gaudy trunks in horror. This wasn't a trip to the supermarket. It was my first surf contest, an event that would attract all the local surfers. Including the Stingrays. Including Cutter.

"Mom, please don't let him—" I began. But when I saw the disappointed look on her face, I stopped myself. Just moments ago, she'd said: *All we ask is that you give each other a chance.*

I decided to pay attention, especially since I was getting off easy—no punishment for the trick I'd pulled with Ariel. I forced myself to smile. "You look killer, Cos," I said. "Just awesome."

Cos grinned, kicked off his trousers, and headed for the door. "Come on, family!" he bellowed. "Let's go watch Megan win that surf contest!"

ELEVEN

Ariel's Diary

Such a peculiar day. One moment I experienced the most joy I have known on this planet. The next moment, I was filled with anxiety and confusion.

I must recount on paper my afternoon at the Playa Vista Surf Tournament. Then later, when my father is out, I will contact Ffffoopp and discuss all with him.

The day began promisingly. After my father and Kathy Larsen resolved their differences, Kathy, Megan, Mickey, and the beast called Gnarly headed for Pelican Point in their red Jeep. Daddy and I followed in our secondhand Volkswagen. As we journeyed, we snacked on helium from our balloons. But we still felt hunger, so Daddy opened the valve on the helium tank in the back-seat. The car filled with life-giving helium, which we con-sumed bountifully.

My pleasure increased when we arrived at the beach and as I viewed the glorious swells rolling toward shore.

Oh, how they reminded me of TubeWorld back home! I gazed at the water, willing myself to become a part of it. But alas, the only water I could produce was in my eyes.

We exited our cars and Megan went to register for the contest. Then Mickey approached and asked, "Why do you suck on balloons? Are you aliens from a planet that likes helium?"

Fear made my metabolism accelerate. Apparently, Mickey had been watching us out of the rear window of the Larsen vehicle.

"Mickey, once and for all, please listen to me," Kathy Larsen said. "Space aliens don't exist."

"Oh, yeah?" Mickey said. "Then why do Cos and Ariel suck helium? And how come they never go to the bathroom?" He turned to me. "Come on, Ariel, what planet are you from?"

I felt myself tremble. No human had yet noticed that my father and I do not use the white porcelain bowl found in Earth bathrooms. How could we? Daddy designed us without bladders or bowels. (Human waste elimination was not dealt with on the medical TV shows he studied). However, since our human bodies are constructed of Zircalonian molecules, we are able to absorb Earth food in the same manner that we absorb helium, and eliminate waste by burping.

"We use the bathroom," my father answered. "It's just that out in the countryside of northern Canada there weren't many bathrooms. So we learned to hold it a long time."

"Yes, and as for the helium, I am doing a science report for school," I said, repeating what Megan had suggested during that first dinner at her house.

"There, that's settled," Kathy Larsen said impatiently. "Now, stop pestering Cos and Ariel."

Mickey nodded and ran off to play along the rocky cliff, but I knew he was not convinced. Is it possible he will uncover the truth about us? My molecules cringe at the thought.

I walked with Kathy, Megan, and Daddy to the ocean. There Megan spied her friends Tara and Robin, and left to converse with them. Also present were Cutter Colburne, Heather Harper, and their companions. They greeted me warmly, and I learned that many of the boys were competing in the surf contest.

Then Megan left Tara and Robin and came to join us. When she observed me conversing with the boys, she immediately grew cold and sarcastic toward me. It was then that I remembered the words she had spoken the night we baby-sat Mickey together: *Cutter Colburne is mine, and don't you forget it.*

I stepped back to allow Megan to stand next to Cutter, but he followed me and continued to converse with me. He caught my eye, smiled, and did not turn to greet her. Could it be, I wondered, that Megan had lied about her commitment to Cutter?

I felt confused, and once again I lamented my inability to perceive minds. But before I could contemplate the matter further, the contest began. By asking questions, I soon learned the rules of the tournament. Male and female surfers aged twelve to eighteen were to compete in three events, called heats. Each heat involved four surfers. Cutter was in the second heat, and Megan the third. The winners of each heat would surf off against each other.

As the first heat began, Cutter and Megan walked down the beach to practice their surfing maneuvers in the water just beyond the contest barriers. After they left, I hit upon the idea of asking Heather about their relationship.

"Cutter doesn't have a steady girlfriend," Heather told me. "Why? Are you interested?"

"I am simply curious," I replied.

Heather smiled in a way that led me to believe she did not trust my intentions. "I wouldn't worry about Megan," she said. "She's not the type of girl the Stingrays go for."

"What type is that?" I inquired.

"Don't worry," Heather replied. "You're it."

I contemplated her answer with great confusion. I could perceive no way in which I am similar to Heather and her friends, except that we both inhabit human female bodies.

But then I remembered my father telling me that my human form is beautiful to other humans. I observed the Stingrays' girlfriends more carefully and realized our physical forms are indeed similar. All of us have yellow hair, unblemished skin, regular facial features, and curving bodies.

That is when an idea occurred to me. Perhaps Earth creatures pay so much attention to physical beauty because they are unable to change their shapes. Surely, if they could transform themselves into any form, their fascination with outward appearances would quickly wane. Undoubtedly, it is this ability that inspires Zircalonians to worship mental rather than physical attributes.

While I was processing these thoughts, the second heat began. Heather and I stood on the beach, watching Cutter compete. Despite his solid form and his need to rely on a surfboard to move through the water, I had to admit his movements were surprisingly fluid and graceful.

When it was announced that Cutter had won his heat, I joined the other observers in clapping heartily. Cutter noticed my enthusiasm and came close. He spoke loudly and foolishly, boasting of his performance. I was unimpressed with his noise and brash movements, so different from the way he behaved in the ocean.

Then the third heat began, and Megan paddled out. She was the only female and drew much attention from the crowd. As she flew through a tubing wall of water, I once again felt a terrible homesickness. Cutter noticed my tears and asked what was wrong.

"At home I used to surf without a board," I explained.

"You mean bodysurf?" he asked.

"What is bodysurfing?" I asked.

"Riding a wave without a board," he answered. "You know, just using your body."

My spirit rose like a winged creature. "Can you teach me to bodysurf?" I asked.

Cutter looked confused. "But I thought you said that's what you did back home—" Suddenly he stopped and smiled. "I mean, sure, Ariel, anytime."

"Now," I said, forgetting that I should have been watching Megan and applauding her performance. Instead, I took Cutter's hand and led him into the surf beyond the contest barrier.

At first my human body felt heavy, awkward, and cold. But with Cutter's help (and my past experience at TubeWorld) I was soon floating.

Next Cutter led me to the breaking waves. He showed me how to wait for the water to rise beneath me, then to paddle and kick until I felt the force of the wave push me forward.

I observed him closely, then duplicated his movements. How simple it was, and how beautiful! Within seconds, I had left Cutter far behind and was plunging toward the shore, propelled by the green water that surged all around me.

"Oh, glorious liquid!" I cried, overwhelmed by bliss. I closed my eyes, and for a brief moment, I felt my solid Earth form melt away. I was changing shape! I was becoming liquid!

The moment ended as quickly as it came. The wave collapsed, and my body—solid once more—was flung face first into the sand.

I looked up to find Megan, surfboard in hand, glaring down at me. Immediately, a feeling of remorse enveloped me. I had come to Pelican Point to support Megan as she surfed. Instead, I had learned to become liquid with Cutter, a boy with whom she longed to form a commitment.

"Megan, did you win the heat?" I asked.

"Like you care," she sneered, turning away.

"But I do," I said, rising and following on her heels. "I was wrong to—"

"Flirt shamelessly with a guy you know perfectly well I'm crazy about?"

"I was not flirting," I answered. "I was overcome by a desire to learn to bodysurf. Cutter helped me."

"Oh, like I should believe that? If you wanted to learn to bodysurf so much, why didn't you ask me?"

"I did not think you would want to help me," I said. "Since we first met, you have treated me always with disrespect and disdain."

"Me?" she cried. "You're the one who walks around with your nose in the air, acting like you're so much better than everyone else. Well, you're not! You're just a shallow, boy-crazy, stuck-up weirdo with an eating disorder!"

Megan's words angered me. Had I not spoken with honesty? Why, then, did Megan respond with cruel fury? But then I realized it had always been thus. I thought back to the time she threatened to blow wind at me, how she laughed at my fear, how she often treated me with contempt.

At that moment, Cutter came out of the water to join us. "Megan, I missed your heat," he said sheepishly, avoiding Megan's eyes. "How'd you do?"

"What do you care?" she demanded. "You've got Beach Bunny Barbie to keep you company."

I did not understand Megan's words, but I perceived clearly the emotion in them. It was then that a new feeling swelled within me. I desired to hurt Megan. And I knew just how to do it.

I looked deep into Cutter's eyes and smiled exactly the way I'd seen Heather and her girlfriends do. "Thanks for the bodysurfing lesson," I said. "Let's do it again sometime." Then, forcing myself not to gag, I leaned forward and touched my lips to the flesh of his right cheek.

Cutter looked stunned, Megan looked crushed, and I was delighted...for a moment. But I soon regretted my actions. Would Cutter now think I wished to commit to him? Would Megan's misery interfere with her surfing? Would our fight destroy the harmony our mutual families now enjoyed?

I felt bewildered. So I returned to the only place on Earth I've found that allows me to feel peace—the ocean. With extreme concentration, I discovered I was able to reproduce my earlier semiliquid state. As I surged forward with the waves, my arms and legs, and occasionally the entire lower half of my torso, briefly lost solidity.

Oh, joy and good cheer! Have my sessions with

Serena begun to bear fruit? Perhaps I am regaining my ability to transform my shape. If so, can mind perception be far behind?

I must continue my pondering later. My father is leaving to see Kathy Larsen. Now is my chance to contact my beloved. Dearest Ffffoopp, I miss you so!

TWELVE

As we drove away from the surf tournament, Mickey leaned over to me and whispered, "Now I'm sure Ariel and Cos are aliens. Wanna know why?"

I let out a groan. Mickey's goofy spaceman theories were the last thing I wanted to hear right now. I was still stewing over my fight with Ariel.

"After your first heat, I saw Ariel bodysurfing," Mickey whispered. "And guess what? Her arm disappeared!"

"Disappeared?" My brother was going crackers.

"Yeah," said Mickey. "It sort of faded into the water. Like her arm turned into the wave."

"What are you two whispering about?" Mom asked as she slowed down for a turn.

"Nothing," I said before Mickey could get started. "Mom, what did you think of that last wave I caught in the finals?"

"Outstanding. Your performance was awesome." She grinned. "Second place in your first contest. In my first few contests, I never placed higher than third."

"I guess I just like competing more than you did," I said, which was true. But what Mom didn't know was that I'd had an extra dose of motivation in the finals. You see, I was surfing against that two-timing Cutter, and I wanted to plow him under.

Okay, okay, so Cutter didn't exactly two-time me. I mean, it's not as if we were going steady or anything. We weren't even dating. But I really liked him, and I had thought he was starting to like me, too.

Which is why I was eager to make Cutter eat sand. I almost did, too. But he caught some mind-blowing air on his last wave and wound up beating me by only two points. What a bummer.

Mom couldn't stop talking about my surfing—and about the mother-daughter interview we'd given after the contest to the reporter from *Surf Scene*. Normally, I would have been flying high, but right now I had other things on my mind. Like how to get Ariel out of my life forever.

The solution came to me when we got home and Mom pushed the playback button on our answering machine. My dad's voice filled the room.

"Hi, kids. Hi, Kathy. I just landed a big job and things are going well, so I'm sending a little extra money this month. I'll call soon, kids. Bye."

Mom laughed. "That dad of yours really comes through sometimes." She took a soda from the fridge.

"Remember that time he won a thousand dollars in the lottery and he took us to Hawaii?"

I nodded. "And the way he blindfolded us and drove us to the airport. We didn't know where we were headed until we were on the plane."

She chuckled. "We never knew what was going to happen next with your dad. He was a real wild card."

I looked at Mom's smiling eyes, and then suddenly it hit me: She was still in love with Dad. Well, maybe not in love exactly. After all, Dad could be pretty irritating sometimes.

For every month Dad sent us extra money, there were two or three months when his child support check was a little short. Or when it didn't come at all.

On the other hand, Dad had a way of making his bad points look appealing. He was handsome, exciting, a rebel with wavy brown hair and a crooked grin. Under the right circumstances, Mom might just fall for him again—at least long enough to make her show Cos and his pain-in-the-butt daughter the door.

I ran to the phone to call Dad. Somehow I had to convince him to come for a visit. But as I dialed, I thought of a way to make my plan even more foolproof. Only it meant involving Ariel.

I paused, thinking it over. The way things were going, I felt more like pushing Ariel in front of a bus than talking to her. But if I wanted to pull off my plan, I'd have to get her involved. So I took a deep breath and called her.

"Hey, Ariel," I said when I heard her voice, "guess what?"

There was a long pause. "What?"

I peeked in the living room to make sure Mom couldn't hear me. "I figured out the perfect way to make our parents fall out of love," I said.

"I will do nothing more to help you," she answered. "I do not like to see our parents fight."

"This doesn't have anything to do with fighting," I said. "In fact, just the opposite. All we have to do is get my mother and your father interested in other people. Then they'll fall out of love with each other and presto—our troubles are over."

"Does this plan involve deceit?" she asked.

"Well, not exactly," I hedged. "All we have to do is arrange things so our parents accidentally-on-purpose meet someone new and exciting. Or, in my mom's case, old and exciting."

"What do you mean?"

"I think my mom still has feelings for my father. So I'm going to invite him here and see what happens."

"And you want my help?" she asked.

"That's right. You must know someone your dad is at least a little attracted to. Is your mother remarried yet?"

There was a long pause. "My mother's molecules were fatally separated many seasons ago."

It took me a few seconds to figure out what that meant. Then it hit me, and I wondered why Mom or

Cos had never mentioned that Ariel's mom had died. "Gee, I—I'm sorry," I stammered. "I didn't mean—"

"Do not apologize." She was silent a moment. Then she said, "I think I know someone to whom my father might develop an attraction."

"No kidding. Who?"

"Our condominium superintendent, Serena Soo. She is graceful and calm with a harmonious nature."

For some reason, Ariel's words irritated me. What made this woman more appealing than my mother? But then I reminded myself it didn't matter. After all, I did want Cos to fall for someone else, didn't I?

"Sounds good," I said. "Now, how do we get them together?"

"I believe Daddy has invited all of you to dinner this Saturday," she replied. "Perhaps we could ask your father and Serena to join us?"

I hadn't considered putting all four of them together, but it made perfect sense. If Mom had a chance to compare Cos and Dad side by side, she might finally figure out what a wacko Cos was. And if Cos could see Mom next to this Serena lady—well, maybe he'd decide Mom just wasn't his type.

Now I just had to figure out a way to convince my father to come for a visit. But how?

The solution, it turned out, was handed to me on a silver platter. Thirty seconds after I hung up, Mom walked into the kitchen and said, "I put Mickey to bed. He's not feeling well."

"What's wrong?" I asked. "He was fine earlier."

"I don't know. He said his stomach hurts and he feels hot. I think he's coming down with something."

That's when the idea hit me. I'd call Dad Saturday morning and tell him Mickey was in bed with a mysterious illness—and asking for his father. If that didn't get Dad here, nothing would.

By the next morning, Mickey had come down with a full-blown stomach virus. He spent the week in bed, watching *Star Trek* reruns. By Saturday, he was all better. But I didn't mention that part to my father.

"Mom told me not to bother you, but I'm worried," I whispered into the phone. "Mick keeps asking for you, and he says he's going to leave me his ray gun. Dad, do you think he's going to die?"

"I'm leaving right now," Dad promised.

Unfortunately, by dinnertime that evening, he still hadn't arrived. I tried to stall, hoping he'd show up, but Mom had her own explanation for my dawdling.

"I know you're annoyed at Ariel," she said. "Cos told me he saw you two arguing during the surf contest. But avoiding her isn't going to help, Meg. You need to talk things over face to face."

When I didn't respond, Mom practically shoved me out the door. I barely managed to slip a note under the mat, telling Dad where we were.

We arrived at the condo a few minutes later. Cos answered the door and we walked in to find the place strewn with children's party decorations. There were crepe-paper streamers hanging from the ceilings, HAPPY BIRTHDAY and MERRY CHRISTMAS banners on the walls, and a wild assortment of party favors on the table. And, of course, balloons of every shape and color were bobbing in the air.

"What are we celebrating?" Mom asked with amazement.

"Nothing," Cos replied. "I just wanted an excuse to buy this stuff. Doesn't it look festive?"

Mom laughed. "Cos, you are too much."

She gave him a hug, then walked into the kitchen to put the dessert she had made in the refrigerator. A moment later, Ariel came out from the bedroom.

"Serena will arrive shortly," she said quietly. "Where's your father?"

"I don't know. He said he'd be here, but—"

The doorbell rang, and Ariel opened the door. A tall Asian woman with waist-length black hair stood there. She wore a gauzy caftan and a necklace of shimmering crystals. I could see right away why Ariel liked her—she looked like a total space cadet.

"Ariel, my dear," she cooed, "I wish you peace."

Ariel looked positively overjoyed. "Come in, Serena," she said in her musical voice.

"Welcome!" Cos bellowed, grabbing her hand and shaking it energetically. "I'm Cosmo Cola. You can call me Cos."

Serena looked a little overwhelmed. "Yes, I've seen you at the mailboxes," she said.

A moment later, Mom walked in from the kitchen. "Ariel wanted to invite her new friend to dinner," Cos explained. "Serena is our condo superintendent."

Serena looked Mom up and down and frowned. "Your aura is strangely clouded. Do you meditate?"

Mom laughed. "I surf. That's better."

"Communing with the water spirits is very healthful," Serena said, "but it doesn't replace meditation. May I suggest—?"

Her words were cut off by a loud knock at the door. Cos opened it and there was Dad, his motorcycle helmet in his hand and a worried look on his face.

"Brett!" Mom exclaimed. "What in the world are *you* doing here?"

"Where's Mickey?" he asked anxiously. "He's not in the hospital, is he?"

"The hospital?" Mom cried. "What are you—?"

"Daddy!" Mickey exclaimed, pushing aside a cluster of balloons to run into his arms.

Dad hugged Mickey hard, then turned to me. "Megan," he said, his eyes flashing, "you've got some explaining to do."

THIRTEEN

"Mickey's fever broke just a few hours after I called you, Dad," I said quickly. "The little guy's still weak, but he's okay now. Isn't that wonderful news?"

"You called your father?" Mom asked. "Why?"

"Mickey asked for him. He was really upset."

"I was?" Mickey asked.

"You don't remember? You must have been delirious." I turned to Dad. "The poor kid was hot as an oven."

"He had a stomach virus," Mom said. "What do you expect?"

"A stomach virus!" Dad cried. "Megan acted as if he was dying."

"I thought he was," I said. "Honest. Anyway, as long as you're here, why not stay for dinner?"

"Yes, please do," Cos broke in. He stepped forward and gave Dad one of his bone-crushing handshakes. "I'm Cos Cola, Kathy's fiancé."

"Fiancé!" Dad exclaimed, pulling his hand away. He turned to Mom. "When did *this* happen?"

"It was kind of sudden," she said. "I was going to write to you."

"Well, I darn well hope so," Dad growled. "If my kids are going to have a stepfather, I want to know about it."

"And a stepsister," Cos said cheerfully. "This is my daughter, Ariel." Ariel smiled in her usual dreamy way. "And this is her friend, Serena Soo," Cos added.

"Greetings," Serena said, looking Dad over as if he were a thoroughbred at a horse auction.

Dad shot her his lopsided grin. He seemed to be calming down. "Hi, Serena," he said.

"Dinner ought to be ready by now," Cos announced, hurrying into the kitchen and returning with some casserole dishes full of blue, green, and yellow glop. "Why don't we all sit down?"

We walked to the dining room table and sat— Mom, Cos, and Ariel on one side, Dad, Serena, and me on the other, and Mickey on the end.

"What's with the decorations?" Dad asked.

"Colorful, aren't they?" Cos replied.

"Forget the decorations," I said. "What's with the food?"

"Doesn't it look yummy?" Cos exclaimed. "I got the recipes out of a magazine—tuna casserole, scalloped potatoes, cauliflower with cheese sauce. But it all looked so bland. So I decided to add food coloring." He grabbed a dish and dumped some bright yellow glop onto his plate.

"What an interesting idea," Serena said. "Very creative. Are you a Scorpio?"

"I don't know," Cos replied. "What's that?"

Serena began explaining astrology while Cos listened attentively. Ariel and I exchanged a satisfied look. Things were getting off to a good start.

"What's your sign, Kathy?" Serena asked. "Since you and Cos are getting married, you might want me to do your charts."

"Look, Serena," Mom said, "I don't want to hurt your feelings, but I don't believe in that New Age stuff."

"I'm not surprised," Serena said coolly. "Your aura is extremely dense. Very unevolved."

Mom wasn't smiling now. "I'm not so unevolved that I can't recognize rubbish when I hear it."

Serena stared at Mom. Mom stared back. "Dad," I said loudly, "tell us about your new job."

"I'm a welder on a skyscraper that's going up in Sacramento. Good money, and I'll be busy all winter." He turned to Cos. "What's your line of work?"

"I used to be involved in...uh...exploration," Cos said hesitantly. "That is, mining. Well, not mining, exactly. More like chemical engineering."

"In outer space?" Mickey asked hopefully.

Cos laughed as if that were the funniest thing he'd ever heard. "Of course not. In northern Canada."

"You mean the territories?" Dad asked. "I've been there."

"You have?" Mom asked with surprise.

"Sure. Remember? I told you about that summer my uncle took me hunting in Canada. We stayed on Great Slave Lake. You know it, Cos?"

"Oh, of course," Cos replied, taking a bite of green tuna. "I used to go scuba diving there a lot."

Dad frowned. "Diving? In that freezing water?"

Cos laughed uncomfortably. "Did I say diving? I meant...uh...sailing."

"Is that where Ariel got blown into a tree by the tornado?" Mickey asked.

"They don't have tornadoes up there, Mickey," Dad said. "The climate isn't right."

"But Cos said—" Mickey began.

"Did I say that happened in northern Canada?" Cos broke in. "That was during a vacation to...uh... uh...southern Canada. Har, har, har!"

"I don't think you know what the heck you're talking about," Dad said irritably. He turned to Mom. "How much do you know about this guy, Kathy?"

"What do you mean?" she asked.

"If you want my advice, you'd better do a little checking to make sure he's on the level."

Mom stiffened. "Thank you, Brett, but I don't need your advice," she said. "In case you've forgotten, we're divorced."

"Oh, dear, I'm sensing a lot of hostility around this table," Serena broke in. "Why don't we all hold hands and do some deep breathing?"

Dad looked upset. "I've got my kids to think about," he said. "I don't want some lowlife running off with the money I send to Kathy."

"Brett," Mom broke in angrily, "you've got some nerve!"

But if Cos was offended, he didn't show it. "Oh, do you send money to Kathy?" he asked. "I think that shows a very generous nature."

I could tell by the open expression on Cos's face that he was sincere, but Dad didn't take it that way. "Okay, so maybe I'm not the most reliable guy in the world," he said gruffly. "At least I hold down a decent job. You still haven't told me what you do."

"Cos works at the surf shop with Mom," Mickey said. "Sometimes he stands in the window and models the new wetsuits."

Dad stared at Cos. "Are you serious?"

"Why not?" Mom asked. "People stop, they smile, they come inside. It's fun."

"It's weird," Dad muttered.

"Thank you," Cos replied happily, as if he'd just received a big compliment.

"Hey, are you making fun of me?" Dad demanded, leaning over his plate and glaring at Cos.

Suddenly, Serena closed her eyes and began to chant. "Ommmmmm," she hummed. "Ommmmmm. All together, people. Let the healing begin."

Cos laughed with delight. "Ommmmm," he boomed. "Ooh, I like that!" He turned to Dad. "Try it, Brett. It'll make your lips tingle."

Dad pushed his chair back and stood up. "I'll make your lips tingle, buddy."

What a disaster! Things weren't turning out the way I'd planned at all. I glanced over at Ariel, who was sitting frozen in her chair, staring at her lap. Obviously she wasn't going to be any help. If anyone was going to save this dinner party, it had to be me.

"Hey, folks, how about some dessert?" I cried.

"Good idea!" Cos exclaimed, pushing back his chair.

We both rushed toward the kitchen at the same time and collided at the end of the table. Cos leaped backward to avoid hurting me, lost his balance, and fell back onto Mickey, who toppled off his chair and burst into tears.

Dad was there in an instant, grabbing Cos by the front of his Hawaiian shirt. "You big ox!" he shouted. "How dare you hurt my kid!"

Cos frowned. "Please remove your hands from my clothing," he said. "Mickey needs our help."

Of course, by now Mom had run over to Mickey, who wasn't really hurt anyway. But Dad was too angry to notice. "Make me," he growled.

"Okay," Cos replied. He put his hands under Dad's armpits and lifted him up like a rag doll. Then he deposited him a few feet away.

Dad responded by taking a swing at Cos. Serena shrieked, Cos ducked, and Dad fell forward across the table.

"I'm bleeding!" he cried. There were three red holes in his thumb where a fork had stabbed him.

"Come to my condo," Serena cooed, hurrying to

his side. "I have some herbal cream that will do wonders for that." Dad hesitated. "Come along, now," she said, sweetly but firmly. She slipped her arm through Dad's and led him to the door.

"Kids, I'll stop by before I leave," he grumbled over his shoulder.

As soon as they were gone, Mom turned to me and said, "What in the world were you thinking, calling your father like that? It wasn't about Mickey, I'm sure of that. So what was it?"

"I'm sorry," I said. "I thought maybe you and Daddy still had feelings for each other."

"Oh, Meg. Not by a long shot. In fact, watching your father make a fool of himself tonight just reminded me how happy I am to be with a nice guy like Cos."

I had to agree with her. My father had behaved badly. But through it all, Cos had been his usual goofy, friendly self. As if to prove it, he smiled at Mom and said, "Now, Kath, don't be too hard on Megan. She loves her father. Think how difficult it must be for her to see you with another man."

Mom thought about it, then turned to Ariel, who was still sitting at the table, looking stunned. "And how tough it must be for Ariel to see you with another woman." She walked over and sat beside her. "Are you all right, Ariel?" she asked.

Ariel nodded slowly. She looked like a sleeper waking up from a bad dream.

"Come on, kids," Cos whispered, motioning

Mickey and me toward the kitchen. "Let's break out the dessert."

It was Angel's Breath Pie, Mom's one and only homemade dessert. It consisted of a graham cracker crust with a sweet, frothy filling that's so light it practically dissolves on your tongue.

I carried the pie to the table and cut everyone a piece. Ariel looked at her plate with her usual lack of interest. But when she touched a forkful of Angel's Breath to her tongue, her eyes lit up. "It's so light, so airy! Why, it's almost gaseous!"

That didn't sound like a compliment to me, but Ariel was practically beside herself with joy. "This is the first food I've enjoyed since I arrived here," she said. "Oh, Kathy, will you teach me to make it?"

Mom looked pleased. "Of course I will," she said.

We ate the entire pie within minutes. Then Ariel turned to me and asked, "Would you go bodysurfing with me sometime?"

I gazed at her skeptically. "You want *me* to go with you?"

She nodded. "More than anyone on Earth."

It seemed hard to believe, and I considered asking her about Cutter. Had they had a fight? But I didn't really want to know. Besides, I was feeling pretty wrung out. If Ariel wanted to make up, I wasn't going to argue.

"Okay," I said. "Maybe sometime next week."

Just then, there was a knock at the door. Cos opened it and there stood Dad and Serena, all smiles.

"Cos," my dad began, "I want to apologize for what happened. It was a misunderstanding, that's all." He held out his hand.

Cos took Dad's hand and pumped it vigorously. "Come in and join us," he boomed.

"No, thanks," Serena said. "Brett and I are going out for a drink at my favorite organic juice bar."

"I'll drop by the house tomorrow, kids," Dad said. He smiled. "As long as I'm here, I figure I might as well get a motel room and stay a day or two." He and Serena exchanged a meaningful glance. Then they said good-bye and left.

"Well, girls, your matchmaking seems to have worked," Mom said with a laugh. "Just not exactly the way you planned it."

Cos slipped his arm around Mom's waist and said, "I think everything turned out wonderfully."

I looked at Cos and my mother standing side by side. I guess I was getting used to it, because I found myself thinking they looked pretty good together—happy, content, like they really belonged.

I shrugged. "Yeah, things turned out just fine."

FOURTEEN

Ariel's Diary

Darkness and gloom! Misery and despair! Ffffoopp is no longer my beloved. Water falls from my eyes, reminding me of our disagreement. And so I relive every thought, every feeling. And so I remember...

I had spent the afternoon bodysurfing at Pelican Point with Megan Larsen. Each time I was out of her sight, I concentrated with all my spirit, willing myself to become liquid. And yet, despite the fact that I have been meditating with Serena every day without fail, I was not as successful at becoming water as I had been last weekend with Cutter. My arms and legs grew liquid with ease, but no matter how much I applied myself, my torso remained solid.

Why? I asked myself. And then I recalled the large helium snack I had ingested in the car with Daddy just before my first bodysurfing experience. I had not repeated this event prior to my afternoon with Megan. On the contrary, hours had passed since I'd last sucked helium, and I had arrived at the beach feeling a tad weary.

I returned home from Pelican Point much excited by my theory. Could it be that helium—not meditation—is the key to reawakening my transformational abilities? I wondered. If so, could huge doses of helium revive my ability to perceive minds as well?

After first assuring myself that Daddy was not at home, I retrieved the ComBox and contacted Ffffoopp. Eagerly, I shared my thoughts with him and awaited his comments.

But much to my dismay, Ffffoopp did not respond with delight or even empathy. Instead, he informed me that bodysurfing on Earth could never offer the same joy as a frolic at TubeWorld.

Me: It is true that bodysurfing is only a pale imitation of TubeWorld. Still, until I return to Z-6, I must find joy wherever I can.

Ffffoopp: Do not delude yourself, Ssweezle. You will never return home. You are an Earthling now.

Me: Do not think such thoughts! Somehow, someday, I will convince my father to return.

Ffffoopp: Your attempts have been futile. You have communicated that to me most clearly.

Me: Then I will return by myself.

Ffffoopp: We both know you are not educated in the science of space travel. You could not reassemble the ship or navigate it back to Z-6. Your only hope is to contact the HEC and ask them to come for you.

Me: But what if the story of the Zircalonian who was

forced to live out his days as a lug nut is true? I could not live knowing I was responsible for bringing such misery upon my father.

Ffffoopp: It is as I suspected. Your mind is growing increasingly Earthly. You no longer perceive the universe like a true Zircalonian.

Me: What do you mean?

Ffffoopp: You accept your father in human form and allow him to live as an Earthling for his own selfish pleasure. You splash with humans and grow tolerant of their ways. You do not please me anymore, Ssweezle. I prefer Turrkel.

Me: Turrkel! What traits does she possess that I do not?

Ffffoopp: Unlike you, she is here on Zircalon-6, not a dozen galaxies away. Together we become liquid, play mind games, float above the purple plains. Ssweezle, perceive me well. I cannot commit myself to a ComBox transmission.

(I wished to reply but could only flash random images of sorrow, anger, pain.)

Ffffoopp: Farewell, Ssweezle. I wish you well. I will communicate your whereabouts to no one.

Me: Ffffoopp, wait! Ffffoopp, my beloved—

But the transmission had been terminated.

A week has passed. I keep imagining Ffffoopp splashing with Turrkel at TubeWorld. And then I remember our very first ComBox transmission. Even then, Ffffoopp had communicated with me concerning his interactions with

Turrkel. Even then, they had made waves together.

My human form stiffens with anger. Could it be that Ffffoopp had committed himself to Turrkel even before Daddy brought me here to Earth? Perhaps the two of them were playing mind games while I was biding my time on GrRp, or even before.

Is Ffffoopp capable of such a thing? It seems impossible. Yet we have been apart so long, with only a ComBox to transmit our thoughts. Who knows what transpired within his mind?

I have begun ingesting increasingly large doses of helium. My father wonders what has caused this great need in me, but I feign ignorance. I know he disapproves of my desire to regain my innate Zircalonian skills and wishes for me to live as a human. But I cannot. So despite my guilt, I hide my intentions and suck deeply from the helium tank.

My theory is correct! After a large dose of helium, I am able, with extreme concentration, to transform approximately seventy-five percent of my body into liquid. Oh, wet and wondrous delight!

Alas, my molecules will not accept larger doses of helium than those I am currently ingesting. When I try, my body merely releases the excess through a series of loud and offensive burps. Which means that as long as I am on Earth, I will never be able to completely transform myself into liquid—at least not the way Ffffoopp and Turrkel can.

Oh, fie! Why did I write the human symbols for their despicable Zircalonian names? Perhaps it is because I cannot stop myself from contemplating them together.

Increasingly, I grow convinced that my affection for Ffffoopp was misplaced. Certainly he was a pleasing companion while I remained on Z-6. But his commitment failed to withstand the demands of time and space.

Another week has passed, and I have spent many delightful hours immersed in the ocean. Sometimes I go bodysurfing with Megan and her friends. Other times I journey to the water alone.

After swimming out beyond the buoys, I transform myself into liquid and allow the ocean to transport me where it will. It is a peaceful, pleasing experience, quite different from the giddy highs of TubeWorld, and yet satisfying in its own right.

On land, I privately practice transforming myself into other states. So far, I have not come close to the success I've achieved in the water. After a large dose of helium, I can will myself to grow slightly gaseous. My skin becomes pink and misty, and the boundaries between my body and the air begin to fade.

At other times, I practice twisting and stretching my body into various useful shapes. Today, for example, I succeeded in elongating my arm so I could recline on my bed and simultaneously reach out to turn off the light switch beside the door.

I can only sustain such activity for a few seconds, and I soon collapse in exhaustion. Still, it provides me with great joy and a sense of accomplishment. And to my surprise, I find that since I've dedicated myself to expanding the boundaries of my transformational abilities, I no longer contemplate Ffffoopp as often.

Even more startling, when I do contemplate him, my emotions are surprisingly flat. Could this be a result of my increased helium intake? I do not know, but it satisfies me most greatly.

A momentous event has occurred! This morning, when my father told me he was going to the store, I replied, "I think there is a half-consumed box of Colonel Crunchy breakfast cereal in the cabinet above the toaster."

"How did you know what I wanted to buy?" Daddy asked with surprise.

"I...er...just a good guess," I told him. But that was a lie. The truth is, I had perceived his thought. At least, I think I had. It's been so long since I last perceived another's mind that I do not remember exactly how it feels. All I know is that without trying, I was aware of my father's desire for Colonel Crunchy.

Oh, delirious ecstasy! Is it possible that my ability to perceive minds has returned?

It's true! I can once again perceive minds! My ability blossomed suddenly at the Larsen household, as my father and I entered the front door and I was set upon by the beast called Gnarly.

As always, I was able to read the dog's tiny mind like

a billboard. "Ariel!" it shouted. "Come play! Throw ball! Come!"

I was shoving the creature off me when I suddenly perceived that Mickey was disappointed in me. He loves Gnarly and wants me to love him, too.

And then I picked up my father's thoughts. He was contemplating Kathy Larsen's face, and his mind was full of love.

Within seconds, I realized I could perceive Megan's thoughts, too. In fact, all the minds in the room were open to me. I could perceive them simultaneously, effortlessly, just as I had done on Z-6. My spirit soared at this overwhelming revelation, and I sent messages of greetings and joy to everyone.

But of course, they did not respond. It was then that I realized our communication was one-sided. I could perceive their thoughts, but they could not perceive mine. Sadly, I was still alone.

My disappointment soon faded, however, as I reveled in my newfound ability. For the first time since I arrived on Earth, I was able to perceive the human mind. And, oh, the things I learned! Mickey is not to be feared, as I once thought. His suspicion that we are aliens is merely a hopeful fantasy, a childish dream. He cannot prove anything, and he would not harm us even if he could.

Even more illuminating is the mind of Megan Larsen. She is not the cruel and heartless creature I suspected. Yes, she is headstrong and quick to jump to conclusions, and she cares too much what others think of her. But her thoughtless actions are mostly a result of her fear of change. And yet, despite her worries, she is growing fond of my father, and increasingly tolerant of me.

And then there is Kathy Larsen. Her mind is open and trusting, generous and kind. She truly loves my father and delights in his enthusiasms. She doesn't always understand him, but that does not seem to trouble her. She accepts him as he is and feels joy in his presence.

Ah, what fascinating revelations! And there are more to come. How eager I am to perceive the mind of every Earthling I meet. Now, at last, I will be able to understand them, and as a result, understand what they expect of me. The possibility thrills me because it means that perhaps I will finally discover a place for myself in this alien world.

But wait. Am I deluding myself? Perhaps I am asking too much. I will never really be an Earthling. And this spinning green and blue ball will never be my home.

And yet, barring a miracle, I must accept the fact that I will not be returning to Z-6. If learning about human beings and perhaps even becoming more human myself can help me find peace here, then surely it is a worthy goal.

FIFTEEN

"Have you been doing extra studying lately?" I asked Ariel as we walked into the school cafeteria.

A few weeks had passed since the dinner party, and our families had been getting along amazingly well. That weekend we were planning a trip to Wild River Amusement Park.

"Not really," she replied. "Why?"

"You aced that pop quiz in social studies," I said.

Ariel smiled mysteriously as we took a seat across from Tara and Robin. "It was easier than I expected."

"Easy!" Robin cried, opening a carton of yogurt. "It was impossible."

"There will be a surprise quiz in math tomorrow, too," Ariel announced suddenly. "Ten problems involving percentages and long division."

"Who told you that?" I asked.

"Er...er..." she muttered.

"What did you do, Ariel?" Robin asked with a laugh. "Read Hayvenhurst's mind?"

"Ooh, that would come in handy," Tara said, nibbling on a carrot stick. "I would love to know what's on Raleigh Easton's mind."

We all turned to look at Raleigh. He was sitting at a nearby table, talking to Cutter and eating a peanut butter and jelly sandwich.

"He's wondering what is wedged between his back molars," Ariel said matter-of-factly. "He hopes his little sister didn't place something unpleasant in his sandwich in order to get revenge on him for accidentally riding his bike over her turtle."

We all laughed. "What an imagination you have, Ariel!" Robin exclaimed.

"No kidding," I agreed, gazing at her thoughtfully as she opened her lunch bag and unwrapped a piece of Angel's Breath Pie—practically the only thing I ever saw her eat these days.

"Here comes Cutter," she announced. I looked up to see him strolling toward us. The closer he came, the louder my heart pounded.

"Hi there," he said, leaning on the table next to Ariel and gazing into her flawless violet-blue eyes. "I'm surfing in a contest down in Ventura this weekend. How'd you like to—?"

"Why don't you ask Megan to go with you?" Ariel broke in. "She didn't know there was a contest this weekend and she desires to enter it."

I couldn't believe my ears! Ariel had voiced exactly what I was thinking. Talk about embarrassing!

"You should enter, Megan," Cutter said casually. He turned back to Ariel. "So, anyway—"

"Why do you fear losing the contest to a girl?" Ariel asked suddenly. "Should not the best surfer win, no matter what her sex?"

Cutter looked stunned. "What?"

"You are worried that if Megan enters the contest, she might win, are you not?"

"Get real," Cutter snapped. He glared over at me. "I beat you before and I can do it again."

Then he looked at Ariel. "I'll call you later, Ariel," he said. He looked a little flustered, which is exactly how I felt.

As he walked away, I turned to watch him. "Yes, Megan, he does look nice from the back, doesn't he?" Ariel proclaimed.

Tara and Robin giggled, but I was too stunned to do anything except gape. Ariel had voiced my thoughts again. I mean, it was almost as if she'd read my mind! But before I could ask her about it, I saw Cutter glance back at us. He was blushing.

"Oh, no," I moaned, sinking down in my chair. "He heard you."

"Why do you wish to crawl under the table, Megan?" Ariel asked. "Are you not pleased with the way Cutter's blue jeans fit in the rear?"

Tara and Robin shrieked with laughter, and some girls at another table turned to stare at us.

"Shut up!" I hissed at Ariel.

Ariel blinked. "Did I say something wrong?"

"Oh, no, of course not!" I told her angrily. "You just humiliated me in front of the only boy I've ever cared about."

"I was attempting to help," she said, hanging her head. But I was in no mood to forgive her.

Okay, so maybe I wasn't totally upset about Ariel's remark. Maybe part of me was upset because Cutter had obviously lost interest in me. But Ariel was the reason for that, too. Wasn't she?

"I don't know which is worse," I finally said to Ariel, "when you try to hurt me by flirting with Cutter, or when you try to help me by telling the whole cafeteria how I feel about his butt!"

"But...but..." Ariel stammered. But I wasn't listening. I stood, grabbed my books, and walked away.

After our scene in the cafeteria, I was in no mood to see Ariel again. But that wasn't possible. Cos had invited us over for dinner, and even though I told Mom I had a pounding headache and a ton of homework, she still made me go.

We arrived at the Cola condo right on time. After we exchanged hellos, Mickey plopped down on the floor, spread out his fleet of toy spaceships, and started to play. I watched Cos sit beside him and begin to play, too, and I realized Cos's personality was starting to grow on me. I didn't find him so irritating anymore. In fact, the sight of him playing with Mickey was kind of touching.

Ariel, however, was a different story.

I walked into the kitchen, where I found her and my mother tossing spaghetti into a pot of boiling water. Ever since the night Mom introduced Ariel to Angel's Breath Pie, the two of them had become cooking buddies.

"I'll start a salad," Ariel said.

"You read my mind," Mom replied. "Check and see what—"

"Lettuce, one tomato, and two carrots," Ariel answered, peering inside the refrigerator.

"Good enough," Mom said. "Do you have a—?" But Ariel had already opened the cabinet and taken out the salad bowl. Mom laughed. "What efficiency!" She glanced at me. "I wish you would help out around the house the way Ariel does."

"I help out," I protested. "What do you want me to—?"

"Set the table," Ariel said.

"Hey, I don't take orders from you," I told her.

"Actually, that's exactly what I was going to ask you to do," Mom said. "Oh, and by the way, didn't your social studies teacher send home a quiz for me to initial? Ariel showed me hers. She got an A."

I shot Ariel a withering look. When had she become such a brown-nose? It was an obnoxious quality, and even worse, it was making me look bad.

I opened the drawer, grabbed a handful of silverware, and headed for the dining room. Ariel followed. "It pains me to perceive that you feel jealousy toward me, Megan," she said.

"Jealousy? What do you mean?" I asked.

"I do not wish to belittle you in the eyes of your mother. Nor in the eyes of your beloved."

"My *what?*"

"Cutter admires your surfing," Ariel continued, "but he prefers to form commitments with females who have yellow hair and curving bodies."

"Females like you, that is," I said disdainfully.

"Yes," she replied. "But in time, he may learn there is more to an individual than outward appearance. I will try to teach him."

"Don't do me any favors," I snapped, walking back into the kitchen. Mom was pouring sauce over the spaghetti.

"That looks delicious," I told her. "I'm so hungry I could eat it all."

Ariel appeared beside me. "Do not," she said. "It will only make your thighs grow larger."

I stared at her, totally stunned. How did she know I've always thought my thighs were too fat? "Shut up!" I shouted. "Just shut up!"

"Megan, that's enough," Mom said. "You've been acting rude to Ariel ever since we got here."

"Maybe that's because I don't like the way she's kissing up to you," I cried. "Or the way she humiliated me this afternoon in front of my friends. In fact, I don't like one thing about her!"

"That's it," Mom said, slamming down the pot of spaghetti. "Go to your room, young lady. You're grounded!"

"What room?" I snapped. "In case you've forgotten, this is Cos's house."

"Then go to Ariel's room," she shot back. "And don't come out until I tell you to."

"But—"

"Go!" she shouted. "Now!"

I stomped away, walked into Ariel's room, slammed the door behind me, and threw myself down on the bed. I lay there for a long time, seething. What injustice! It was Ariel who'd behaved like a jerk, but I was the one paying. It wasn't fair.

I let out a sigh. And to think I'd practically been ready to tell Mom to go ahead and marry Cos. What had I been thinking? There was no way I could survive with Ariel as my stepsister—I knew that now. Somehow I had to find a way to end Mom's relationship with Cos once and for all. But how?

I sat up in bed and looked around, searching for inspiration. I'd failed at turning Mom and Cos against each other, and my plan to make them fall for someone else had been a bust. What was left? Then suddenly it hit me. I had to find a way to make them hate each other's kids!

Immediately, I knew it was a brilliant idea. After all, I told myself, parents love to criticize their own children, but if someone else puts down the little darlings, watch out.

I decided to look around Ariel's room. Not snooping exactly, just checking around for something incriminating. A letter to Cutter filled with nasty lies about me perhaps, or a cheat sheet from today's social studies quiz. Just a little something that would make Mom decide she didn't want Ariel for a step-daughter.

I listened carefully to make sure no one was coming, then quickly checked out Ariel's closet, her dresser, and her desk drawers. Talk about boring! I couldn't find anything except clothes, a few toiletries, and some school supplies. Gosh, I thought, this girl is just as shallow as she seems.

Finally, in desperation, I knelt down and looked under the bed. That's when I saw it—a small box, about the size of a telephone answering machine, only made of a material that looked sort of like frosted glass. I pulled it out and looked it over. There were no words anywhere, no symbols of any kind, no switches, knobs, or dials either. It was as blank and mysterious as Ariel herself.

I turned the box over and noticed a small red button. How could I resist? I pushed it and waited. A series of tiny multicolored lights appeared on the top of the box. They pulsated slowly. The box began to hum.

Now I was a little scared. What was this thing? Hesitantly, I rubbed my fingertip across the lights. Suddenly, they began to flash and change. Patterns appeared so quickly my eyes blurred.

I was just about to put the thing back where I found it when the lights began to flash again. As

I stared at them, they slowly resolved into something that made sense. Words appeared—inside my head!

"Ssweezle, is that you?" they said. I waited, too stunned to move. "This is Ffffoopp, communicating from Zircalon-6, the largest planet in the Tlleekk galaxy. Am I addressing a human being on the planet Earth?"

Then images of a strange alien landscape hit my brain like a 3-D movie. I let out a shriek and dropped the box. It hit the floor with a crash and the lights went dark. All at once, everything made sense—Cos's childlike innocence, Ariel's formal way of talking, their weird habits and attitudes.

"Mickey was right!" I shouted hysterically. "Cos and Ariel are aliens!"

SIXTEEN

Mom and Cos came running when they heard my voice. "What are you yelling about?" Mom asked, flinging open the door to Ariel's room.

I looked at Cos. Suddenly, everything about him seemed bizarre and threatening—his unruly hair, his too-green eyes, his big, bearlike body. How had I ever managed to convince myself this creature was a human being? He was so obviously an alien that my knees began to shake.

"M-Mom," I stammered. "I-I have to talk to you. In private." I pulled her into Ariel's room and closed the door. "Mom," I whispered, "try not to panic when I tell you this." I took a deep breath. "Cos and Ariel are aliens."

Mom crossed her arms and looked at me hard. "This is another one of your schemes to get me to break up with Cos, isn't it, Megan?"

"Mom, please," I begged, "this is serious. Look!" I picked up the box and pushed the red button on the bottom. Nothing happened. "Oh, my God, I broke it!"

"Broke what? What is it?"

"Some kind of intergalactic transmitter. I turned it on and a bunch of lights began to flash. Then words appeared. Only it was like I was thinking them instead of reading them. They said, 'This is Foop from Zirconium-6,' or something like that. Then it asked, 'Am I addressing a human being on the planet Earth?'"

Mom shot me a wry smile. "What did you answer?"

"Mom, listen!" I cried. "This is real. Your fiancé is an alien. For all we know, his human-looking body is nothing more than a disguise. Rip it off and you'll probably find yourself face to face with a green, two-headed space monster!"

At that moment, the door opened and Mickey walked into the room. "What's going on?" he asked.

"Mickey," I said, putting the box on the bed as I knelt down to take his hand, "I'm sorry I didn't believe you."

"Believe what?" Mickey asked.

"Megan, really—" Mom began.

"Mom," I told her, "he has a right to know." I turned back to Mickey. "You were right, Mick. Cos and Ariel are aliens from outer space. I found their transmitter and received a message from their planet."

Mickey's eyes lit up. "I knew it!" he exclaimed. "I just knew it! What did it say?"

"I'll tell you later. Right now we've got to get out of here and call the authorities."

"But why?" Mickey asked.

Poor Mickey. He was just a child—a naive, trusting child who thought all aliens were as sweet and gentle as E.T. But I wasn't so gullible. I'd seen *Independence Day*, and I was prepared for the worst.

Mom started to say something, but she was cut off by a knock on the bedroom door. We all turned as Cos and Ariel walked into the room. "Is everything okay?" Cos asked. Then he saw the box and his mouth fell open. "What's that doing in here?"

"I—I—" I stammered.

Ariel stared at me as if she were looking inside my brain. I froze, suddenly remembering the way she had voiced my thoughts about Cutter before I even spoke them. *Oh, no,* I thought fearfully, *they can read our minds!*

"Megan was looking through our possessions," Ariel said, proving beyond a shadow of a doubt that my theory was true. "She discovered the box and..." Her eyes grew wide. "She received a communication!"

Cos turned to glare at me. "Is that true?"

I gazed up into Cos's enormous face. I'd never seen him so angry. In fact, I'd never seen him angry, period. It made me realize how little we really knew about these aliens. There was no telling what they were capable of. "Uh...uh..." I sputtered.

"Is this what you use to communicate with your

planet?" Mickey asked, picking up the box.

Cos lunged forward and practically ripped the thing out of Mickey's hands. "Don't be ridiculous," he boomed. "This is a new kind of laptop computer. It's being developed by a friend of mine in Canada. He gave me one to try out."

"Mom," I said, trying desperately to think happy, peaceful, please-don't-disintegrate-us thoughts, "tell Cos about that pounding headache you have. Tell him we have to go home. Please."

But Mom seemed to be rooted to the wall-to-wall carpeting. "I have some bad news for you, Cos," she said. "I think Megan broke your computer."

"Oh, despair and desolation!" Ariel wailed. She turned on me and shouted, "You have plagued me from the first moment I met you. I loathe you, Megan Larsen! Do you perceive me? I despise you with every molecule of my being!"

"Ariel!" Mom scolded. "I'm disappointed in you. Maybe both of you girls need to be grounded until you learn to get along with each other."

"Why are you blaming Ariel?" Cos demanded. "Megan is the one who was snooping around in our stuff." He spun around and grabbed my shoulders so hard I winced. "What kind of communication—I mean, e-mail—did you receive, Megan? What did it say? Tell me!"

Why was Cos asking me about the message? Couldn't he read my thoughts? Or did he just want to hear it from my own lips before he grabbed my neck and killed me with his planet's version of the Vulcan death pinch?

"Talk!" Cos bellowed.

"Cos, let her go!" Mom cried, stepping forward to grab his arm. "I know you're upset, but you don't have to act like a Neanderthal."

What was Mom saying? Didn't she realize who she was talking to? "Don't listen to her, Cos," I begged. "Mom was only kidding. I'll tell you about the message. It was from—"

"Megan, will you stop with this foolishness?" Mom begged. She turned to Cos. "Don't pay any attention to her. She's just trying to scare me by pretending that you and Ariel are from outer space."

"What?" Cos gasped.

Mom shrugged. "Apparently it's her latest scheme to end our relationship."

Ariel stared at me and I knew she was reading my mind. "It's not a scheme," she said seriously. "She truly believes it."

Cos laughed loudly—too loudly. "Oh, Ariel, don't be absurd." He turned to me. "Now tell me what that message said and I'm sure we can clear up this little misunderstanding."

I hesitated, uncertain whether I should run or fall to my knees and beg for mercy.

"Megan, don't be scared of Ariel and Cos," Mickey said. "They're good aliens. They won't hurt us."

"Megan," Mom said sternly, "this isn't funny anymore. You're upsetting Cos and Ariel. And look at Mickey. You've got him all excited about something that isn't even true."

Cos's eyes were boring into mine. "What else did you find besides the ComBo—I mean, the computer?" he asked. "Come on, Megan. Out with it."

"Nothing," I said in a small voice. "Honest."

Mickey, completely oblivious to the deadly drama going on in front of him, walked up and tugged on Cos's sleeve. "Now that Megan knows who you are, will you take us for a ride in your ship?"

"Quiet, Mickey," Cos said impatiently.

"Come on, Cos. Please?"

"No!" Cos snapped, wrenching his sleeve out of Mickey's grasp. "I'm talking to Megan."

My skin tingled with fear. "Mickey..." I began in a warning tone.

"At least teach me how to use this transmitter thing," Mickey continued, walking over to pick up the box from the dresser where Cos had laid it.

"Don't touch that!" Cos shouted, shoving Mickey aside as he grabbed for it.

"Cos, be careful," Mom scolded. "You could have hurt him."

"Then take me for a ride in your spaceship," Mickey whined. "Pretty please with a cherry on top?"

"Shut up!" Cos bellowed, holding his ears. "Shut up, shut up, shut up!"

"Cos," Mom said angrily, "don't talk to Mickey like that. What's gotten into you?"

"Why does he insist on thinking I'm an alien?" Cos answered irritably. "It's just stupid!"

"Maybe because you've been playing those foolish games with him," Mom snapped. "You've just been encouraging his outer space fantasies!"

Cos looked confused. "I thought I was supposed to be nice to your kids. Isn't that what you wanted?"

"Is that the only reason you've been nice to Megan and Mickey?" Mom demanded. "Because you thought it was what I wanted?"

"Look, Cos," Mickey exclaimed suddenly, "I got it to work!"

We all turned toward Mickey, who was standing next to Ariel's dresser holding the little box. Tiny lights were flashing across the surface.

"Give me that!" Cos roared. He grabbed the box so violently, Mickey was thrown back against the dresser. Ignoring Mickey, Cos turned to Ariel, eyes flashing. "This thing has caused me nothing but trouble!" he bellowed. With that, he reared back and flung it at the bed as hard as he could. The box bounced into the air and smacked against the dresser, missing Mickey's head by mere inches.

"That's enough!" Mom cried. "First you insult my daughter, then you try to injure my son. I don't know you anymore, Cos Cola."

"I am not an alien!" Cos shouted.

Mom stared at him in amazement. "This is a side of you I've never seen before. The man I met at that surfwear show was gentle, caring, in love with life.

But you—I can't love a man like you. I don't even *like* you!"

Cos looked stunned—or maybe he was just summoning his extraterrestrial powers. "Kathy—"

Mom shot him a look that would freeze the sun. She grabbed Mickey and me by our arms and marched us out to the living room. "Cosmo Cola," she shouted over her shoulder, "I wouldn't marry you if you were the last human being on Earth!"

"Human being?" I moaned. "Don't you get it, Mom? He's not human. He's an alien—a very angry alien who's probably right this minute contacting his planet and telling them to start the invasion."

Mickey burst into tears. "Does this mean I don't get to ride in Cos's spaceship?"

"Not another word!" Mom cried, hustling us out the front door and into our car. "From this moment on, I never want to hear the names Cosmo and Ariel Cola again!"

SEVENTEEN

Ariel's Diary

My life is over. Never in my ninety-nine years have I felt such sorrow, such angst, such desolation.

After Kathy Larsen and her children left our condo, my father traversed the hallway, head hung low. Then he locked himself in his bedroom.

The next morning, he emerged, eyes red and puffy, to announce that he considers himself a failure as a human being. "I thought I could become one of them," he said sadly. "I thought I could stay here forever, living among them, accepted and at ease. But I was deluding myself. I'm an impostor, a fake, and it was inevitable I'd be found out."

"Do not blame yourself," I said. "I am at fault. If I had not disobeyed you and taken the ComBox into my room, Megan would never have found it and activated the preset contact circuit."

Daddy shook his head. "If it wasn't the ComBox, it would have been something else. I'm not a human being and never will be. You tried to tell me that, but I wouldn't listen. Now I'm paying for my lack of judgment. I've hurt the one human I care for most in the world, and my life will never be the same."

I knew that Daddy had not meant to frighten Mickey or Megan, or to hurt Kathy Larsen. It was only shock and fear that made him act so uncharacteristically loud and aggressive.

"Perhaps there is still hope," I said. "Kathy Larsen does not believe we are aliens. And Megan and Mickey do not know for certain. Perhaps they can be convinced that we are truly human."

Then I informed Daddy that I can again perceive minds. "I did not want you to know. I feared you would be angry with me," I explained. "I know you wanted me to behave as human beings do. But perhaps my Zircalonian powers can help us. If I know what humans are thinking, maybe I can persuade them to believe what we wish them to."

Daddy was so overcome with sorrow, he expressed only mild shock at my renewed powers. "It is too late," he said. "Megan has probably called the authorities. There will be reporters, photographers, curiosity seekers. We will never be left in peace. And if they discover the ComBox or our space transport vehicle, I shudder to think what will happen to us."

"We could depart Playa Vista," I suggested. "The Earth is large. There are many places to hide."

Daddy smiled sadly. "You are kind," he said. "I know you don't want to stay here. You never wanted to come in the first place. And yet you would remain on Earth to make me happy." He reached out and gently ran his hand through my hair. "You are a kind and loving daughter."

But were my motives purely unselfish? I must admit they were not, for since I have regained my ability to perceive minds, my understanding and sympathy for Earthlings has grown considerably. Their actions may often be strange and displeasing, but their motives are generally pure and good, and almost always deserving of sympathy. Knowing that, I can no longer remain aloof and withdrawn, especially from the humans with whom I have grown most intimate.

Daddy's thoughts assailed me, bringing me back to our present predicament. He said aloud, "We will leave this condo immediately and move into a motel. There we can live anonymously while I reassemble our space transport vehicle. When it is ready, we will leave Earth at once."

"And return to Zircalon-6?" I asked. I was surprised to discover that I was not at all certain I wanted the answer to be yes. I missed my home greatly, it is true, but could life on Z-6 ever be the same for me now? I pictured myself at TubeWorld, observing Ffffoopp as he joyously made waves with Turrkel, and I felt sorrow.

Even more troubling was the image of my father, living life as an eccentric outcast, unable to exist in a socially acceptable state of gaseousness and serenity. Would he be jeered at? Punished? Forced to function as a lug nut? The possibility filled me with dread.

"I was never happy on Zircalon-6, and never shall be," Daddy said. "Therefore, I have decided to live out the rest of my days roaming the universe in search of helium and selling it to the Helium Exploration Corps on a freelance basis."

Oh, woe! Oh, weariness! My father's answer, although not what I had feared, brings me no peace. From this day forth I will be without soul mates either Zircalonian or Earthling, alone except for my heartbroken father, aimlessly wandering through the vacuum of space.

Now I sit alone in my bedroom, sadly waiting for my father to return from Serena Soo's condo, where he is informing her that we are moving out.

Oh, how I long to go bodysurfing with Megan, then sit upon the warm sand and consume a generous slice of Angel's Breath Pie with Kathy while my father and Mickey build spaceships in the sand. But these Earthly joys are henceforth to be only melancholy memories, for I am soon to leave this benign and pleasing planet, never more to return.

EIGHTEEN

I woke up the next morning with the sun in my face. Gnarly was snoring peacefully at the foot of the bed. Then, in a rush, it all came back to me: Cos, Ariel, intergalactic transmitter, aliens from space!

With a gasp, I jumped out of bed and headed down the hall, searching for Mom and Mickey. They weren't in their bedrooms.

"Mom!" I screamed. "Mick, where are you?" By the time I'd made it to the living room, I was certain they'd been abducted. By now they were probably a hundred light years from home, on their way to Cos and Ariel's planet!

Then it hit me. Mom hadn't been abducted. She was working at the store. Most Saturdays, she took Mickey with her.

I threw on some clothes, grabbed a granola bar, and headed out the door. As I pedaled my bike to High Tide Ocean Sports, I tried to decide what to do next. The way I figured it, the more miles we put between us and the aliens, the better. That meant we had to do it fast. Then once we were away, I planned to contact the authorities, the media—anyone who would listen—and tell all.

I hopped off my bike with a sigh. Just having a plan—no matter how uncertain—made me feel better. Now I just had to convince Mom to take us on a trip. "Mom," I called, flinging open the door to High Tide, "guess what?"

Mom looked up from behind the cash register, where she was sitting with her head in her hands. "What?" she asked glumly.

"I just called SurfLine," I lied. "There's an epic swell heading for Mexico. If we leave now, we can fly to Baja before the crowds show up."

Mom let out a weary sigh. "Why bother? There are waves right here in town, if anyone cares."

I stared at her. Never in my life had Mom passed up a chance to surf an awesome swell. Last year she closed the store and took Mickey and me out of school when she heard that record-breaking surf was pounding Hawaii's North Shore.

"Mom, come on," I urged. "A surfing safari will do you good. It'll get your mind off...you know."

"Don't worry about me," Mom said sadly. "All that matters now is you and Mickey. That's why I've decided we need some family therapy."

"What?"

"I never knew how much I was neglecting you."

"Neglecting me? What do you mean?"

"All your ranting last night about aliens. I never

understood how much you needed attention—"

"Mom, we don't need therapy, we need—"

Just then, the door opened and Mickey walked in, feet dragging and head hung low. His eyes were red and he looked as if he'd been crying. But when he saw me, he perked up.

"Megan!" he exclaimed. "Let's go in back and play with my spaceshi—" He stopped, then said quickly, "I mean, my blocks."

Something was up, I realized. Mickey's spaceship was his favorite toy. "Okay," I said, "let's go."

We walked through the door that said EMPLOYEES ONLY and went into Mom's office. "What's wrong, Mickey?" I asked. "You look miserable."

"I *am* miserable," he said. "Mom won't let me call Cos and Ariel. She doesn't even want me to say their names, or talk about aliens, or play with my spaceships, or anything. Plus, she told me she's taking us to family therapy. What's that?"

"It's a place to talk about your problems with a counselor," I explained.

"What problems? I don't have problems. I just want to see Cos and Ariel. What's wrong with that?"

"Mom and Cos broke up, remember?"

"That's because you told Mom that Cos and Ariel are bad aliens," Mickey said with a pout. "But Mom misses Cos, and I'll bet he misses her, too. Why don't you tell the truth? Cos and Ariel aren't bad. They're nice."

"How can you be so sure?" I asked. "We don't

know why they came to Earth or what they want from us or anything."

"I don't care," he said in a shaky voice. "I love Cos. He's going to be my new daddy."

"Cos can't be your daddy," I said. "Don't you understand? He's not even human."

Mickey's lower lip began to tremble. A huge tear hung on his eyelashes. "It's all *your* fault," he sniffed. "Everything was going great till you found that stupid transmitter thing. Now Cos and Ariel hate us, and Mom thinks we're crazy."

Gosh, I felt awful. I didn't want to make Mickey unhappy. I tried to remind myself that everything I was doing was for his own good. "Cheer up," I said, putting my arm around his shoulders. "All we've got to do is convince Mom to take us on a trip. When we come back, everything will be back to normal."

Mickey's eyes lit up. "You mean, Mom and Cos will get married?"

"Uh...no. I mean, things will be back to the way they were before Mom met Cos. Just you, me, Mom, and Gnarly—one big, happy family."

The tear rolled down Mickey's cheek. "I don't want that family," he sobbed, pushing my arm off his shoulder. "I want Mom to marry Cos."

"Come on, Mickey," I said, "don't get so worked up. Let's play with your—"

"I don't want to play with you!" he wailed. "I hate you!" Then he turned and ran out the door.

NINETEEN

"Mickey, wait!" I called, running after him. But he was already gone.

"Where's Mickey off to?" Mom asked. "He looked upset."

"Home probably," I said. It was only a few blocks away. "And he *is* upset. He doesn't want to go to family therapy, and neither do I." I leaned over the counter and looked her in the eye. "Come on, Mom. All we need is a change of scenery. What do you say? A few weeks in Baja?"

"A few weeks!" Mom exclaimed. "Who's going to watch the store? No, let's drop it. And if you want to hang around here, make yourself useful. Fold some T-shirts. Go on, get busy."

I spent the rest of the morning working and trying to convince Mom to leave town. But nothing worked. By the time noon rolled around, I realized it was time to come up with another plan, but what? I decided to head for home and think it over.

* * *

I unlocked the door and walked inside, bracing myself for Gnarly's greeting. But nothing happened— no click-click of nails on the floor, no earsplitting barks, no slobbering licks. No Gnarly.

"Gnarly?" I called. "Where are you, buddy?"

No answer.

"Mickey, are you here?"

Silence. I walked through the rooms, looking for them. At first, I figured Mickey had grabbed Gnarly and gone into hiding somewhere. "Come on out, Mick," I called. "Let's talk."

But when I got to his bedroom, I knew something had happened. Mickey's floor, usually littered with toy spaceships and *Star Trek* action figures, was completely empty. I checked the stacking bins against the wall. They were empty, too.

Now I was getting nervous. I opened Mickey's closet. His *Star Trek* backpack was missing, and so was his *Star Wars* sleeping bag.

"Mickey!" I shouted, trying to ignore the sick feeling in the pit of my stomach. "This isn't funny. If you're hiding, you'd better come out now."

But deep down, I knew he couldn't hear me. The aliens had taken him. He was gone!

I ran to the phone and called the store. "Mom," I said, so frightened that my words came out in one big jumble, "you've got to come home. The aliens have abducted Mickey."

"Megan, slow down," Mom said. "What are you talking about?"

I told her about the missing backpack, the sleeping bag, and the toys. "Gnarly's disappeared, too."

"Relax," Mom said. "Mick probably went over to Travis's house. You know they love to camp out in his treehouse."

"In the middle of the day? Mom, listen to me. Cos and Ariel took Mickey."

"Megan, use your head. Do you see signs of a struggle?"

"No, of course not. Do you think Cos would need to use force to convince Mickey to go with him? All he'd have to do is offer him a ride in his spaceship and Mick would skip out the door."

"Good Lord," Mom said, "you're more traumatized than I realized. Maybe I'll call that therapist right now."

"Mom, listen to me," I pleaded. "You've got to call the police. They'll listen to you."

"There's no reason to call the cops yet," Mom answered. "I'm going to phone a few of Mickey's friends. If I don't find him, I'll close the store and drive around the neighborhood. Stay put and I'll call you as soon as I know anything."

"But Mom—"

"Sit down and relax. I'll call you soon." Then she hung up.

Sit down and relax? Stay put? Was she crazy? Creatures from outer space had abducted my little brother and I was the only one who knew it.

Obviously, I had to find him, not to mention Gnarly. Provided they were still on Earth, that is.

I hopped on my bike and pedaled at top speed to the Colas' place. When I reached the entrance to their condominium complex, I hid my bike in the bushes and walked to the back of their building.

Dropping to my hands and knees, I began to crawl cautiously toward Ariel's bedroom window. Inch by inch, I moved closer, then pulled myself up to peer inside.

Empty! Ariel's bedroom was completely empty. No furniture, no clothes, no nothing. I crawled to Cos's window and looked in. His bedroom was empty, too. Jumping to my feet, I ran to the complex directory and located Serena's condo. Then I jogged over to it and rang her bell.

"They moved out this morning," she said, brushing incense ash from the sleeve of her purple and green caftan. "No forwarding address. They wouldn't tell me where they were headed."

My head was spinning. *They've left the planet!* my brain screamed. *They're gone, and they've taken Mickey with them!*

"You know, I want to thank you for setting up that dinner," Serena said, oblivious to my growing hysteria. "Your father and I really connected that night. We've been calling each other every day, and I'm going up to visit him next weekend."

I turned and ran, not bothering to reply. What did

it matter if my father and Serena the Space Cadet were falling in love? What did anything matter now that Mickey was gone?

I leaped on my bike and pedaled to the store. Mom was just locking up. "They're gone!" I cried, squealing to a stop in front of her. "Cos and Ariel moved out this morning."

Mom didn't seem to be listening. "He's not at any of his friends' houses," she said with a worried frown. "Put your bike in the Jeep. I'm going to drive around. Maybe he's roller-skating at the park."

"Mom, he's not at the park," I cried. "He's with Cos and Ariel. They're probably halfway to their planet by now."

"Megan, that's enough!" Mom snapped. "I don't want to hear another word about Cos and Ariel. This is serious. Your brother is missing and we're going to find him!"

Mom looked so furious I was afraid to answer. Besides, what good would it do? I lifted my bike into the Jeep and climbed into the front seat.

We spent the next three hours driving around, searching for Mickey. I knew darned well we wouldn't find him, and of course we didn't.

Finally, Mom headed for home and called the police. They promised to alert the officers on duty to keep their eyes peeled for a six-year-old boy carrying a backpack and a sleeping bag, accompanied by a large sandy-colored dog. If they didn't find him by dark, Mom was supposed to file a missing-person report.

As the hours dragged on and Mickey didn't show up, I found myself growing more and more hysterical. I couldn't think straight, and I began to wonder if I was wrong about Cos and Ariel.

But if Cos and Ariel were normal human beings, how was I supposed to explain the intergalactic transmitter and the weird message I'd received? Could it be I'd hallucinated the entire thing?

The thought scared me. I walked to the bathroom and looked in the mirror. The girl that gazed back at me didn't look insane. But then how does insane look? I wasn't really sure.

At five o'clock, Mom called the police again. Ten minutes later, two officers showed up to take a missing-person report. When they asked me about Mickey, I didn't even mention Cos and Ariel. I just felt too confused. But that didn't stop Mom from talking about them. She told the officers all about her relationship with Cos, and she explained about the fight they'd had the night before.

"Mickey was very upset when we left the condo," she said. "He loves Cos."

"Have you talked to Cos since Mickey disappeared?" asked one of the officers, a woman with short blond hair.

"I called him," Mom replied, "but there was no answer."

"Cos and Ariel moved out this morning," I said. "The condo super told me."

Mom seemed to be hearing me for the first time. I guess she'd just been too upset to take it all in when I told her earlier outside the store.

"Moved out?" she repeated with a bewildered expression. "But where would they go?"

The second police officer scribbled something in his blue notepad. "There's a chance this Cos fellow kidnapped your son and your dog, hoping to get back at you for breaking up with him," he said.

"No," Mom said, shaking her head. "I can't believe it. Cos wouldn't do a thing like that."

"You'd be surprised what a jilted lover will do," the blond officer said.

"But—" Mom began.

"We're going to need a recent photograph of Mickey," the female officer said gently. "And we want you to tell us everything you know about Cosmo Cola."

"I—I don't know much," Mom said haltingly. "Cos was always a little mysterious about his past."

The two officers shot each other a knowing look. The male officer leaned forward, pen poised over his notepad. "Let's start from the beginning, Mrs. Larsen," he said.

An hour later, the sun dropped behind the trees, setting the houses aglow with its orange rays. A strong wind was coming up, shaking the leaves and sending garbage cans clattering down the street. Mom had returned to the police station with the officers to look over some mug shots, on the off chance Cos might be a wanted criminal. I was standing at the living room window, watching dark storm clouds roll across the gray-blue sky.

"You'd be surprised what a jilted lover will do," the blond officer had said. But what about a jilted alien? There was no telling what one of them might be capable of. That is, if Cos really *was* an alien. I wasn't sure anymore.

I closed my eyes and tried to imagine where Mickey might be. Was he in the backseat of Cos and Ariel's VW, rumbling down the interstate on the way to who-knows-where? Or was he sailing beyond the reaches of human space, on his way to their planet?

Tears filled my eyes and I blinked to get them out. That was when I noticed a person standing motionless on the sidewalk across the street.

I blinked again, then leaned my forehead against the window to get a better look. My heart seemed to stop, then it revved into overdrive. I was looking straight at Ariel Cola—and she was looking back at me!

TWENTY

My head was spinning. Ariel hadn't left the planet. She hadn't even left Playa Vista. And that meant there was a chance that Mickey hadn't left, either!

I was so excited I forgot to be scared. I turned from the window, threw open the front door, and ran outside into the windy twilight. But when I got there, she was gone.

Good heavens, I thought, *did I hallucinate her, too? Maybe I really am insane!*

A light rain had begun to fall. Suddenly, I saw something moving in the bushes beside the house across the street. An instant later, Ariel took off across our neighbor's lawn.

I ran after her. "Ariel, stop!" I called. "Where's Mickey?"

When she heard that, she hesitated and turned slightly. I saw my chance and took it. I lunged forward and knocked her to the ground.

"Where's my brother?" I demanded, pressing her against the damp grass.

"What do you mean?" she asked. "Is he not with you?"

"You know darn well he isn't," I said angrily. "Now where is he? Come on, talk or I'll squish your creepy alien face into the mud!"

Ariel craned her neck to look up at me. When I met her intense violet-blue eyes, the reality of what I was doing hit me. I was threatening a creature from outer space. Or was she? I had to know.

"Ariel, I know you're probably going to pulverize my brain in about two nanoseconds, but before you do, please tell me the truth. Are you or are you not a space alien?"

"Let me up," she said. I hesitated, then rolled off her. Slowly, she sat up and pushed her wet hair off her face. "I am Ssweezle from the planet Zircalon-6," she said softly.

It was true! "Have you come to destroy us?" I asked nervously.

She shook her head.

"Invade us?"

She shook her head again.

"Perform mind experiments on our puny humanoid brains?"

"Hardly," she replied in her musical voice. "My father and I came to Earth to live as human beings. You see, when Daddy was working for the Helium Exploration Corps, we were stationed on GrRp. There he viewed television transmissions from Earth and fell in love with your planet. From that day forth, he was determined to reside among you."

So Mickey was right. Cos and Ariel really were good aliens. Or at least harmless...unless Ariel was lying. "Why didn't you tell me this before?" I asked suspiciously.

"We were afraid that if our true identities were discovered, we would no longer be able to live among you in anonymity. But now that is of no consequence, for we will soon leave your planet."

"You're leaving? But what about Mickey?"

"We did not kidnap Mickey," she said. "My father is heartbroken about the fight he had with your mother. He would never think of taking Mickey to get back at her."

I stared at Ariel in astonishment. I hadn't said a word about kidnapping or the cops' theories about Cos taking Mickey to punish Mom. So how did she know I suspected him of doing just that?

"Simple," she said, answering my unspoken question. "I can read your mind."

"I knew it!" I cried. "I just knew it!"

"On my planet, everyone can perceive thoughts. But when we arrived on Earth, my father and I lost our ability. I regained my powers recently—I still do not know why—but my father has not."

My brain was reeling. I was talking to an alien. A mind-reading alien. Of course, I had suspected as much ever since I found their transmitter. But to actually hear it from Ariel's own mouth—well, it was mind-boggling, to say the least.

"Wha—what did you want?" I stammered. "I mean, why were you standing outside our house?"

Ariel let out a wistful sigh. "Unlike my father, I have not adjusted easily to life on your planet. But when Daddy informed me that we were leaving Earth, I was startled to find myself filled with a peculiar sense of melancholy. I will miss this planet, Megan—the warm sand, the blue sky, the surging ocean waves. But most especially I will miss the people—your mother, your little brother, the boys and girls at school. In truth, I will even miss you."

Normally, Ariel's backhanded compliment would have made me furious. But at that moment, I was too stunned to feel anything but amazement. "You mean, you came back to say good-bye?" I asked.

"My father warned me not to leave our motel room, but I could not stay away. I do not know what I hoped to find. I only know I had to return one last time...to look....to remember..."

I gazed at Ariel's unhappy face, trying to make sense of things. Could it be I'd been wrong about her? Maybe she wasn't an annoying, insensitive boyfriend stealer or a cruel, brain-sucking space invader. Maybe she was just a confused kid trying to deal with all the changes life was throwing her way. In short, maybe she wasn't all that different from me.

I was still trying to wrap my brain around that concept when I heard a click-click on the other side of the street. I turned to see Gnarly, his hair wet and matted, trotting down the sidewalk. "Gnarly!" I cried, leaping to my feet. "Here, boy!"

As soon as he heard my voice, he came running. Then he spotted Ariel. Ignoring me, he leaped on her and happily licked her face.

"Blech!" she cried. "Begone, beast!"

"Gnarly disappeared at the same time as Mickey," I told Ariel, grabbing his damp collar and pulling him off her. "Too bad you can't talk, buddy. You might be able to help us."

"He doesn't need to talk," Ariel announced. "I can perceive his thoughts."

"You mean it works on animals, too?"

Ariel looked into Gnarly's brown eyes. "I perceive sand. Large waves. The beach."

"But Mom and I already searched Pelican Point this afternoon. Mickey wasn't there."

"Wait a minute," Ariel said, holding up her hand. "I see rocks," she said. "Climbing inside cliffs. Does that make sense?"

"The caves in the cliffs!" I cried. "Mickey loves to play there during low tide. Maybe he's hiding in one of them."

"Did you not investigate the caves this afternoon?" Ariel asked.

"We checked out the ones where he usually plays, but we didn't walk around the point. The tide was starting to come in and—oh, no!" I moaned. "With this storm blowing through and the tide coming in, the waves will be huge. Last time that happened, the caves were completely flooded. The lifeguards found a dead coyote inside one. They said it must have gotten trapped and—"

"Megan!" Ariel cried, understanding. "We must find him!"

I ran back to the house and quickly scribbled a note to Mom telling her where I was headed. Then I wheeled my bike out of the garage and motioned for Ariel to climb on behind me. She grabbed my waist and we took off, barreling through the rain with Gnarly running along behind.

When we got to Pelican Point, we dumped the bike in the parking lot and ran across the beach to the cliff. The rain was coming down in sheets now, and the tide was rising. Thick, grinding waves were wrapping around the point. The largest ones crashed against the sand just a few yards from the cliff, sending surging water into the caves and spraying white foam high into the air.

Gnarly barked twice, then ran into the water and paddled toward the point. Forgetting all about Ariel, I plunged in after him and began swimming through the frigid surf.

Suddenly, I saw something moving out of the corner of my eye. I turned to find Ariel swimming effortlessly beside me, her long blond hair streaming behind her.

"Stick together!" I shouted, reaching through the whitecaps to take her hand. That's when I realized she didn't have a hand, or an arm, either. In fact, her entire torso had completely disappeared!

"If I ingest ample portions of helium, I can partially transform myself into a liquid or gaseous state," she explained. "Fortunately, I had a large meal before I came to your house."

I tried to speak, but no words came out. Gnarly picked that moment to let out a series of shrill yelps. I spotted him out near the point, trying to climb onto some partially submerged rocks. Each time he managed to drag himself out of the water, a wave came and flung him back into the surf.

"Come on!" I called to Ariel, and we headed for the point. Suddenly, I noticed something bobbing in the water. It was Mickey's *Star Trek* backpack! I swam harder.

The tide was still coming in, and by the time we reached the point, the waves were breaking right on the cliff. My heart sank. Any caves that were there had to be filled with water, I was sure of it. Plus, it was so dark and rainy, I could barely make out Gnarly's head bobbing above the water. How were we ever going to find Mickey?

"Megan!" a small voice called. "Megan, help!"

My heart leaped into my throat. It was Mickey! But where was he? Gnarly barked, as if trying to answer my question. But it was Ariel who understood. "Look!" she exclaimed, pointing up at the cliff face. "Up there!"

I looked up to see Mickey clinging to the side of the rocky cliff. He was at least twenty feet up, with his feet wedged against a narrow outcropping of rock and his hands clinging to a tangled root that grew from a crack in the cliff. Each time a wave broke, sea spray splashed up at his shivering body.

"Jump, Mickey!" I called, treading water. "I'll catch you!"

He looked over his shoulder. "I'm scared!"

"Do not be afraid," Ariel called. "We are here to assist you!"

Mickey looked again, then shook his head. "I—I can't!" he wailed. "The waves are too big!"

Just then, a rock broke loose from the top of the cliff and tumbled down the side toward Mickey. He let out a frightened wail and cowered against the cliff. The rock bounced past him, missing his shoulder by inches.

"Mickey, hurry!" I cried. "If you jump, we can catch you. If you fall..." My voice trailed off as I pictured Mickey landing on a submerged rock.

"I'm scared!" he cried again.

"Mickey, I'm coming to get you!" Ariel shouted suddenly.

"But how—?" I began. The words died in my throat as I watched Ariel's arm transform from water back into flesh. She raised it toward Mickey. Higher...higher... I let out a gasp. Her arm was stretching like a rubber band! Mickey stared with amazement as her arm wrapped gently around his waist like a life preserver. Then slowly it shrunk back to normal, bringing Mickey down with it.

The instant Mickey touched the water, Ariel let out a groan and collapsed backward. She floated there, face up and eyes closed. I swam to Mickey and scooped him up in my arms. "What's wrong with Ariel?" he cried. "Make her wake up!"

I shook her, but she didn't move.

"Grab her!" I shouted over the sound of the surf and rain. "We'll tow her in."

Mickey clutched the sleeve of Ariel's blouse. "I've got her," he said.

The tide was still coming in, and the waves were getting bigger. With Mickey and Ariel in tow, I began the long swim back to shore.

TWENTY-ONE

As we neared the shore, I heard a familiar voice.

"Megan! Mickey!" my mother cried. "Oh, thank goodness!" A moment later, she plunged into the shorebreak to meet us and I felt her warm arms hugging us tightly.

"Megan and Ariel rescued me," Mickey said through chattering teeth.

"Ariel?" Mom asked with alarm, gazing down at her motionless body. "Oh, no! What happened?"

"Ariel stretched her arm like Silly Putty to get me down from the cliff," Mickey said. "Then she fainted or something."

Mom didn't bother to reply. Instead, she lifted Ariel into her arms and asked me, "Can you make it in without help?"

My legs and arms felt like rubber, but I nodded, and she hurried ahead with Ariel. I grabbed Mickey and staggered through the surf. When we finally collapsed on the sand, Mom was giving Ariel mouth-to-mouth resuscitation.

"Is she going to be okay?" I asked, wiping the sand and rain off my face.

Mom glanced up with a worried frown. "It's weird. Her skin is warm and pink, her heart is beating, but I can't get her breathing." She exhaled three more breaths into Ariel's lungs, then jumped to her feet. "Megan, get over here and keep working on her. I'm going to call an ambulance."

While I knelt beside Ariel, Mom ran across the beach to the pay phone.

"What's wrong with her?" Mickey asked. "Why won't she wake up?"

"I don't know," I gasped between breaths. "If she really hasn't been breathing, her skin should be cold and blue but..." I frowned, looking at her soft pink cheeks. "It's just not normal."

"That's because Ariel isn't normal," Mickey pointed out. "She's an alien."

As usual, he was right. There was no point in treating Ariel like a drowned human being. If we wanted to save her, we had to think like Zircalonians. But how did Zircalonians think?

That's when I remembered what Ariel had said to me earlier: *If I ingest ample portions of helium, I can partially transform myself into a liquid or gaseous state.*

"Helium!" I announced. "That's what she needs."

Mickey understood immediately. "Some kid had a party on the beach this afternoon," he said. "I watched it from the cave. There were balloons."

We ran off across the pitch-black beach toward the picnic tables. Sure enough, there was still a bunch of wet, wrinkled balloons tied to the benches. I grabbed them, and we hurried back to Ariel.

I knelt down beside her and ripped the ribbon off one of the balloons. I held her nose, shoved the end of the balloon between her lips, and let the helium rush into her mouth. She gasped and coughed. Her eyelids fluttered.

"It's working!" Mickey exclaimed. He untied another balloon and held the end to Ariel's lips. She sucked greedily, then opened her eyes and sat up.

"Many thanks," she said with a weak smile. She reached for the rest of the balloons and inhaled them one by one. "I am recovering nicely now," she told us. "And I am pleased to see that both of you are out of danger as well."

I heard footsteps and turned to see Mom running back to join us. When she saw Ariel, she stopped dead in her tracks. "Ariel, are you all right?"

Ariel nodded. "Thanks to Megan and Mickey's quick thinking."

Mom turned to us. "What happened?"

Mickey was eager to explain. "You see, on Ariel's planet they inhale—"

"I found something stuck in her throat," I interrupted, thinking fast. "A piece of kelp, I think. I pulled it out and she started breathing."

Mom looked impressed and Mickey looked indignant. "That's not what hap—"

Now it was Ariel's turn to interrupt. "Kathy, I think we should let Megan and Mickey change out of their wet clothing. They seem quite chilled."

I'd been too preoccupied to notice until now, but Ariel was right. My teeth were chattering and my feet felt kind of numb. I looked at Mickey. His lips were blue.

"Oh, you poor kids!" Mom exclaimed. "Let's get into the Jeep. Come on."

We ran back to the parking lot and piled into the Jeep. Mom turned on the heat full blast. I lifted my toes to the vent. It felt heavenly!

Ariel turned to my mother. "Would you please phone my father and tell him where I am? He is residing in the Siesta South Motel, room 104."

"Of course I will," Mom said, pulling beach towels out from under the seat. "I'll call 911 and cancel the ambulance, too. Kids, take off your wet clothes and wrap yourselves in these." She handed us the towels and headed back to the pay phone.

As soon as Mom closed the Jeep door, Mickey turned to me. "Why did you lie, Megan?" he demanded. "Cos and Ariel have been sucking helium since we met them. I've seen them."

How could I explain why I'd lied to Mom when I wasn't even sure? "Mick, I've been thinking," I said, trying to get my thoughts straight for myself, as well as for him. "Telling everybody that Ariel and Cos are aliens isn't a good idea."

"But why not?" he asked. "After you found Cos's

transmitter, you couldn't talk about anything else."

"That's because I thought Cos and Ariel were evil aliens. But I was wrong. Ariel proved that to me tonight." I glanced over at her. "She saved your life, Mickey."

"But I still don't see why I can't tell my friends about Ariel and Cos," Mickey insisted.

How could I explain? Then I hit on a concept Mickey was sure to grasp. "Do you remember what happened to E.T. once the government found out about him?" I asked. "They tried to take him away from his Earth family and study him like a bug under a microscope. He was miserable, remember?"

"Those guys were mean," Mickey said with a nod.

"Well, the same thing could happen to Cos and Ariel if everyone finds out they're from Zircalon-6. That's why we can't tell anyone."

Mickey thought it over. "Not even Mom?" he asked at last.

"We can't risk it. I mean, what if she gets hysterical, just like I did? She might call the police to investigate, and when they do—"

"We'll be gone," Ariel broke in. "Have you forgotten, Megan? My father has decided to leave Earth as soon as possible."

"No!" Mickey cried, but I was too stunned to say anything. The fact is, I had forgotten, or maybe I just hadn't wanted to believe it. I mean, it's weird, I know, but my attitude about Ariel had changed.

Partly, of course, it was because she had risked

her life to save Mickey. But it was more than that. Tonight I'd finally gotten an inkling of what it must have been like for Ariel during the last couple of months.

Imagine being plopped down on a new planet and told to act like a normal twelve-year-old Earth girl. Ariel must have felt totally lost, and being forced to deal with me and my take-a-hike attitude must have only made things worse.

I glanced over at her, sitting beside me in the dark Jeep. I wanted to tell her what I was thinking, apologize for treating her so badly, but I felt tongue-tied. And then it hit me. I didn't have to tell her. Ariel could read my mind!

"You can't leave," Mickey insisted. "You're going to be my stepsister and Cos is going to be my step-father."

"But my father and your mother broke up," Ariel said, "and now Daddy feels he's a failure as a human being."

"But why?" Mickey asked. "It wasn't his fault. If Megan hadn't found your transmitter thing and made such a big stink, he and Mom would still be engaged."

Mickey was right, of course, and that gave me an idea. What if we could convince Mom that the whole aliens-from-outer-space story had been just another one of our desperate schemes to break her and Cos up? After all, that had been Mom's reaction to my story in the first place. How hard could it be to convince her she'd been right all along?

Quickly, I explained my idea to Ariel and Mickey. "If it works," I said, "maybe Mom will stop thinking I'm having a nervous breakdown, and Cos won't have to worry about the authorities discovering his true identity."

"And then Cos and Mom will make up," Mickey added eagerly.

Ariel nodded. "And then maybe—just maybe— Daddy will decide not to leave the planet."

At that moment we heard a yelp, and Gnarly's wet face appeared at the side window, carrying a dark, wet something in his mouth. I let out a gasp, then threw open the door. He leaped inside, water flying everywhere, and dropped Mickey's backpack onto the seat.

Just then, Mom opened the back door and lifted my bike into the back of the Jeep. When she saw Gnarly, she did a double take. "What's he doing here?" she asked.

"He led us to Mickey," I explained. "But we lost him in the surf. In all the excitement, I forgot about him."

"Well, he didn't forget us," Ariel said. To my amazement, she scratched his ear and rested her head against his damp neck. Gnarly's tail thumped happily against the seat.

Mom climbed into the driver's seat. "I called your father, Ariel," she said. "I told him I'd drive you home. But first I want to understand what happened today. Mickey, what were you doing here at Pelican Point?"

"I ran away," he said with a pout.

"But why, honey?" Mom asked.

Tears filled his eyes. "Because I love Cos, and if I can't have him for a stepfather, I don't want to live with you anymore."

Now Mom was crying, too. "Oh, Mickey," she sniffed, "I'm sorry. I was so worried about Megan and her outer space fantasies that I guess I didn't pay enough attention to how this whole thing was affecting you. But I'll make it up to you. I promise."

"You mean you're going to marry Cos?" Mickey asked hopefully.

"I—I don't know. I'm too upset to think about that right now. Anyway, who knows if he still wants to marry me?"

"He might," I said, seizing the moment, "if we told him the truth about last night."

"The truth? What do you mean?"

"You thought my story about the intergalactic transmitter was just another scheme to break up you and Cos, remember? Well, you were right. That weird box really was a laptop computer, just like Cos said. But I made up the whole alien story, hoping I could cause enough trouble to start a fight."

"Megan, I'm ashamed of you!" Mom scolded. "Ariel, were you in on this, too?"

Ariel hung her head in a very convincing way. "Yes, I was. But when Mickey disappeared, I realized how hurtful our lies had been. And I realized something else as well." She looked up, her eyes moist and glowing, and I knew she wasn't pretending anymore. "I have grown very fond of you, Kathy. And despite the differences of opinion I have had with your children, I care greatly for them, too."

"I feel the same way about Ariel," I said, and I really meant it. "Sure, Cos and Ariel drive me nuts sometimes, but that doesn't mean I don't care about them." I shrugged. "After all, that's how it is with family."

"Oh, boy! Now you can marry Cos!" Mickey exclaimed, jumping up and down in the seat.

Mom laughed, but there were tears in her eyes. "I suppose I can...I mean, if he'll have me."

"There's only one way to find out," I said, pointing at the car keys in her hand.

Mom started the car and pulled out of the parking lot. "Next stop," she announced, "the Siesta South Motel!"

TWENTY-TWO

Ariel's Diary

Will I ever grow accustomed to Earth people's peculiar ways?

This was my question as I stood barefoot in the sand at Pelican Point, flowers woven into my hair, a yellow dress draped over my solid human body. Megan stood beside me in exactly the same outfit. Mickey was at my other side, hopping from foot to foot in beige pants and a yellow shirt. Nearby, Gnarly romped in the shorebreak, a yellow ribbon tied around his damp collar.

I thought back to the commitment ceremonies I had experienced on Zircalon-6. Traditionally, the happy mates-to-be begin the ritual in a solid state, forming tubular bands that spin and twist in elaborate patterns. Then they transform themselves into liquid and surge together, creating powerful waves. In the final stage, they become gaseous and float together across the purple plains, perceiving each other in fully committed bliss.

But this was not Zircalon-6, it was Earth, and in mere moments, my father and Kathy Larsen would commit themselves to each other in a human wedding ceremony.

I gazed at the ocean, watching the sun rise above the water. Then Daddy and Father Biff, a minister and former professional surfer, walked across the beach from the parking lot. Daddy was dressed in beige shorts and a colorful shirt covered with pictures of surfers and palm trees. His unruly hair was combed and his face was beaming.

My heart swelled with joy. It seemed like only yesterday he had been distraught and despondent, resigned to a life far removed from Earth and all human interactions. And yet, in truth, an entire week had passed since the night we rescued Mickey from the cliff.

How well I recall that night, and our arrival at the Siesta South Motel. When I opened the door with my key, Daddy enveloped me in a bear hug that nearly asphyxiated me. Then he turned to Kathy with an expression that only a human face can display—a mixture of sorrow, regret, tenderness, and love.

That is when Kathy explained that Megan and I had made up the story about the ComBox in order to cause discord between our parents.

"It's true," I said, silently thankful that Daddy could not perceive my thoughts. "Megan made up the whole thing. I went along because I wanted you to end your commitment to Kathy and return to...to northern Canada. But I've changed my mind. I want to stay here. I want you to marry Kathy."

"I—I don't know what to say," Daddy stammered. "Megan, Mickey, do you feel the same way?"

"Yes," Megan said firmly, "I do."

All eyes turned to Mickey. Megan and I knew that one wrong word could destroy our carefully crafted fabrication. "I'm kind of sorry you're not aliens," Mickey said. "But I still think you're pretty special—for plain old humans."

Everyone laughed, Daddy the loudest of all. Then he turned to Kathy and dropped to one knee. "I said it before, and I'll say it again," he proclaimed. "You're the most charming, delicious, mind-blowing human being I've ever laid eyes on. Will you marry me?"

Kathy let out a girlish giggle. "Yes, Cos, I will."

My thoughts returned to the present as Kathy Larsen, wearing a sleek yellow and black wetsuit, caught a wave and surfed it into shore. Then she jumped off her board and unzipped her wetsuit, revealing the yellow dress she wore underneath. She walked to Daddy's side and the ceremony began.

By Zircalonian standards, the wedding ritual was rather dull. Still, when Kathy and my father promised "to love and cherish each other, and to love, cherish, and nurture all three of our children," I was overcome by a surprising elation, which caused my eyes to produce salt water.

I glanced at Megan. She, too, had water in her eyes. Mickey was grinning, and even Gnarly was wagging his tail.

Moments later, the ritual was over and Daddy and Kathy were entwined in an embrace. Then we all hugged each other, and everyone returned to the Jeep to unload the coolers and arrange the food on tablecloths in the sand.

If I had allowed my mind to ponder the momentousness of the event I had just witnessed—my father had married an Earthling, and I had suddenly gained a human stepmother, stepsister, and stepbrother!—I undoubtedly would have been assailed by a multitude of doubts and fears. But I barely had time to unpack the Angel's Breath Pie before the guests arrived for the celebration picnic. They included my new stepgrandmother, Lillian; dozens of Kathy's surfer friends; Megan and Mickey's father with Serena Soo, who was draped over him like a tablecloth; and Tara and Robin.

As the sun rose in the sky, other people unconnected with the wedding arrived at the beach. Among them were Cutter Colburne and the rest of the Stingrays. As I watched, they paddled out to the point and began to surf.

I turned back to the party. Everyone was talking, laughing, eating, throwing Frisbees and dancing to the raucous music coming from Father Biff's boom box. All of a sudden, I felt a little sad and was overcome by a deep need to momentarily distance myself from the noise and excitement, to be alone, to think.

I walked up the beach and turned in the direction of the parking lot. It was then that I saw him—a tall boy, slender and graceful. He stood at the edge of the beach, holding a limp balloon twice the size of a beach-ball with a small box attached to it. Beside him was a helium tank.

I walked closer, intrigued. Then I realized I recognized the boy from school. He was older than me, an eighth grader perhaps. I did not know his name.

Suddenly, he noticed me gazing upon him. "Pardon me," he said in a deep, resonant voice. "Would you mind helping me out?"

All at once my skin began to tingle and I found it difficult to breathe. "What do you want?" I asked.

"Could you please hold this radiosonde while I fill my weather balloon?"

"Wh-what is a radiosonde?" I asked.

"It's an instrument—actually, a group of instruments—that measures and transmits information about temperature, pressure, and humidity in the atmosphere. I plan to send it up with this balloon."

I stepped closer and he handed me the box, which was attached by some kind of filament to the balloon. While he filled the balloon, I studied him. His hands were so white I could see the veins beneath the skin. I found this quite pleasing, as were his pale blue eyes and carefully combed brown hair. His movements were studied and economical. His gray pants and blue shirt were neat and clean.

The boy tied off the balloon and removed it from the

tank. A small amount of helium escaped into the air. I breathed it in deeply. He turned to me. "You go to my school, don't you?"

"Yes," I said. "My name is Ariel. Ariel Cola."

"Mine is Raymond Bartelinsky."

The sound was most pleasing to my ear. With great interest, I perceived his thoughts and learned that he was fascinated by science, especially anything relating to weather, the Earth's atmosphere, and outer space. Even more delightful, I perceived that he found my appearance, my voice, and my actions to be highly pleasant.

"Would you tell me about your weather balloon?" I asked. He looked pleased.

"Sure," he said. "You can help me launch it if you want."

My heart danced inside my chest. Together, we released the balloon into the air. It was attached to Raymond's belt by a thin, clear line that allowed it to rise to a height of two hundred feet. We stood side by side at the edge of the sand, watching it float on the wind, while Raymond talked about meteorology. As he spoke, I gazed into his shining blue eyes, transfixed.

"Ariel!" a voice called, breaking my trance. It was my father. "Ariel, come back. We're getting ready to cut the cake."

"I must go," I said. "I will see you in school, I hope."

Raymond smiled, and my body grew strangely hot and prickly. "You can count on it," he said.

As I returned to the wedding picnic, Cutter emerged

from the ocean and spotted me. He peeled off his wet-suit and walked over. "What's all this?" he asked. "Some kind of party?"

"Just minutes ago my father wed Megan's mother here on the beach," I explained.

"That explains the dress," he said, grinning as he looked me up and down. "Boy, you look fantastic!"

I looked away. No longer did I wish to manipulate Cutter's affection for me in order to cause Megan pain. In fact, I longed to make him understand that I did not desire his attentions. But how?

For weeks, I had tried ignoring him, thinking he would grow tired of me, but alas, my efforts had been a fail-ure—a fact I knew to be true because I was perceiving his thoughts. Indeed, he was still infatuated with my physical form and with my speech and facial expres-sions, which he found mysterious and alluring. Of course, he had no knowledge of my true personality because he could not perceive my thoughts, nor had he made any sincere effort to engage me in meaningful conversation.

"You wanna dance?" Cutter asked.

"Maybe later," I said. Actually, human dancing does not interest me. It is too kinetic and awkward to be pleasing to my Zircalonian soul.

The music ceased and everyone gathered around Daddy and Kathy. Together, they sliced the cake. Then, arms entwined, they fed the first two pieces to each other.

I glanced at Cutter. He seemed to be looking at

Megan, who was standing on the other side of the crowd with Mickey. *Perhaps he is thinking about her,* I thought hopefully. But when I attempted to perceive his thoughts, I discovered I could catch only an inkling. They seemed clouded and distant.

I concentrated with every facet of my mind. Gradually, I was able to glimpse a small portion of his thoughts. That is when I became aware that Cutter was not thinking about Megan. He was thinking about me—with my clothes off!

Without pausing to consider my actions, I raised my hand and slapped his cheek.

"Hey, what was that for?" he cried.

"I am not fond of you, Cutter," I said. "We are incompatible and I wish most fervently that you would leave me alone."

Cutter stared at me. His cheek was red and his jaw was hanging open. Then he turned on his heels and walked away.

The music resumed and everyone proceeded to dance. Megan ran up to me. "What was that all about?"

When I explained, she looked completely flummoxed. Then she frowned. "Wow, and to think I was head over heels for that jerk. What was I thinking?"

I sighed. "Judging by mere appearance is a common human foible."

Megan nodded. "I wish I could read minds like you. If I could, I would have figured out a long time ago that Cutter was a waste of my time, and that you and Cos—" Her voice trailed off. Then she leaned forward and encircled me with her arms. "Oh, Ariel, I'm glad you're my stepsister!"

"As am I," I answered happily. Then I asked, "Megan, do you think it is possible to fall in love with someone the instant you first observe him?"

She shrugged. "I guess so. I mean, that's the way it was with my mom and your dad, wasn't it?"

"That is so." I let out a long sigh. "In that case, I am in love."

"You're kidding? Who's the guy?"

"Raymond Bartelinsky."

She stared at me, eyes protruding. I tried to perceive her thoughts, but to my amazement, they were completely closed to me. I focused my mind on the other people around me, but it was the same thing. Try as I might, I could no longer perceive minds.

And then a startling idea came into my head. Perhaps it is romantic love, not the Earth's atmosphere or some other natural phenomenon that causes the Zircalonian mind to lose its powers here. In truth, when I arrived on Earth, I was in love with Ffffoopp and my mind-reading abilities were nil. When my feelings for Ffffoopp died, my powers returned. Since meeting Raymond, they have disappeared again.

"I must speak to my father," I said, leaving Megan to find him. He was dancing with Kathy. I grabbed his arm and stood on tiptoe to whisper in his ear. "Daddy, when we first arrived on Earth, could you perceive minds? Please, tell me the truth."

"Yes," he said, "but I didn't want to tell you because

you had lost your powers and were so unhappy. But after I met Kathy, I couldn't do it anymore." He smiled, shrugged, then continued dancing.

So it was true. Love had taken away my powers. And yet, oddly enough, I was not forlorn. In fact, I was barely concerned.

Can it be I am becoming more human than I previously realized? It is a shocking thought, yet one that no longer fills me with dread. In fact, if being human means loving and being loved by Raymond Bartelinsky, I am more than eager to proceed.

At that moment, my father took my hand and pulled me toward him. "Let's dance, Ariel!"

Not wishing to displease him, I made an awkward attempt at swaying to the pounding beat. He stretched out his other hand to Kathy. She took it and we began to move together.

I looked around for Megan. She was sitting beside a teenage boy, the younger brother of one of Kathy's surfer friends, showing him the *Surf Scene* article entitled "The Legend Continues: An Interview with Kathy and Megan Larsen." The boy had a friendly, open face, and I was gratified to observe that he listened attentively each time Megan spoke. Then the boy said something, and Megan laughed appreciatively.

Could this be the beginning of a growing bond between them? I wondered. My heart swelled with hope.

At that moment, Daddy shouted for Megan and Mickey to join us in our dance. Soon all five of us were swaying together. Gnarly leaped at our feet, barking and spinning. The guests circled around us, clapping and urging us to proceed.

Megan's father and Serena handed each of us a glass of sparkling apple juice, and Daddy lifted his glass in a human ritual that I later learned is called a toast. "To family!" he cried.

"To family!" each of us echoed.

Megan, Mickey, and I grinned at each other as we gulped down our cider. Then the five of us tossed our glasses into the sand, joined hands, and resumed our joyful dance.